Thomas Edward Brown

Old John

And other Poems

Thomas Edward Brown

Old John
And other Poems

ISBN/EAN: 9783337206871

Printed in Europe, USA, Canada, Australia, Japan

Cover: Foto ©Andreas Hilbeck / pixelio.de

More available books at **www.hansebooks.com**

OLD JOHN

AND OTHER POEMS

OLD JOHN

AND OTHER POEMS

BY

T. E. BROWN

AUTHOR OF 'BETSY LEE,' 'FO'C'S'LE YARNS,' ETC.

London

MACMILLAN AND CO.

AND NEW YORK

1893

The thanks of the Author are due to the Proprietors of the *National Observer* for permission to reprint some poems which have already appeared in the columns of that Journal.

TO

H. G. D.

M. E. D.

THIS VOLUME IS

AFFECTIONATELY INSCRIBED

MARCH 1893

CONTENTS

CONTENTS

OLD JOHN

Old John, if I could sit with you a day
    At Abram's feet upon the asphodel,
There, while the grand old patriarch dreamed away,
    To you my life's whole progress I would tell ;
    To you would give accompt of what is well,
What ill performed ; how used the trusted talents,
    Since last we heard the sound of Braddan bell,
           "A whin bit callants."

You were not of our kin nor of our race,
    Old John : nor of our church, nor of our speech :
Yet what of strength, or truth, or tender grace
    I owe, 'twas you that taught me—born to teach

B

All nobleness, whereof divines may preach,
And pedagogues may wag their tongues of iron,
    I have no doubt you could have taught the leech
            That taught old Chiron.

For so it is, the nascent souls may wait,
    And lose the flexile aptness of their years :
But if one meets them at the opening gate
    Who fans their hopes and modifies their fears,
    Then thrives the soul: the various growth appears,
Or meet for sunny blooms or tempests' grappling
No wind uproots, drought quells, frost nips, blight sears
            The well fed sapling.

Old John, do you remember how you ran
    Before the tide that choked the narrowing firth,
When Cumbria took you ere you came to Man
    From distant Galloway that saw your birth?
    Methinks I hear you with athletic mirth
Deride the baffled sleuth hounds of the ocean,
    As on you sped, not having where on earth
            You were a notion.

What joy was mine! what straining of the knees
　　To test the peril of that strenuous mile,
To hear the clamour of the yelping seas!
　　And step for step to challenge you the while,
　　And see the sunshine of your constant smile!
I loved you that you dared the splendid danger;
　　I loved you that you landed on our Isle
　　　　A helpless stranger.

Old John, old John! the air of heaven is calm;
　　No ripple curls upon the glassy sea:
But, as you wave on high the golden palm,
　　Though love subdues the thrill of victory,
　　You must remember how at Trollaby
Your five-foot-one of sinew tough and pliant
Threw Illiam of the Union Mills, and he
　　　　Was quite a giant.

O wholesome food for keen and passionate hearts,
　　Tempering the fine pugnacity of youth
With timely culture of all generous arts,
　　Rejecting menial tricks and wiles uncouth—

Old John, your soul was valiant for the truth,
But ever 'twas a chivalrous contention:
   Love whispered justice, and the mild-eyed ruth
      Kissed grim dissension.

Old John, if in the battle of this life
   I have not sought your precepts to fulfil,
If ever I have stirred ignoble strife,
   If ever struck foul blow, as bent to kill,
   Not conquer, by the love you bear me still,
Oh intercede that I may be forgiven.
   Stern Protestant—*I pray to saints!* I cry
      To you in Heaven.

Old John, you must have much to do indeed
   If I am all forgotten from your mind.
Absolve me not—I cannot hold a creed
   That would impute you dltst or unkind
   Nor Father Calvin: ask the old man blind
If pointed faith, ask the grim Confession
   Or Angel say what black error lurks behind
      Such intercession.

Old John, you were an interceder here :

 For me you interceded with great cries.

How have I stood with mingled love and fear,

 And not a little merriment !   My eyes

 Beheld you not, Old John ; your groans and sighs

And gasps I heard by listening at the gable

 Inside of which you knelt, and shook the skies—

  But first the stable.

It was a mighty "wrastling" with the Lord :

 The hot June air was feverish with the heat

And agony of that great monochord.

 Our old horse, standing on his patient feet,

 Ripped from the rack the hay that smelt so sweet ;

And, when there came a pause, their breath soft pouring

 I heard the cows ; while prone upon "the street"

  Our swine were snoring.

You prayed for all, but for my father most—

 "The Maister," as you called him—*that on rock*

Of sure foundation he might keep the post,

 And (by a change of metaphor) *might stock*

 God's heritage with vines to endure the shock

Of time and sense, being planted with his planting :
  That so (another trope) of all the flock
        Not one be wanting.

Old John, I think you must have met him there,
  My father, somewhere in the fields of rest :
From doubt enlarged, released from mortal care,
  Earth's troubles heave no more his tranquil breast.
  Oh, tell him what you once to me confessed,
That, all the varied modes of rhetorick trying,
  You ever liked "the Maister's" sermons best
        When he was crying.

Old John, do you remember how we picked
  Potatoes for you in the days of old ?
Bright flashed the *grep*, and with its sharp prong pricked
  The pink fleshed tubers.   We were blithe and bold.
  Dear John, what jokes you cracked ! what tales you
        told '
So garrulous to cheer your "little midges,"
  What time the setting sun shot shafts of gold
        Athwart the ridges.

And when the season changed, and hay was mown,

    You weighed the balance of our emulous powers,

How "Maister" Hugh was strong. the ponderous cone

    To pitchfork ; but to build the fragrant towers

    Was none like "Maister Wulliam." Blessed hours !

The empty cart we young ones scaled—glad riders !—

    And screamed at beetles exiled from their bowers,

        And homeless spiders.

But when the corn was ripe, and truculent churls

    Forbade us as we culled the *cushaged*[1] stook,

Your eye flashed fire, your voice was loosed in *skirls*

    Of rage. Old Covenanter, how could you look

    The very genius of the pastoral crook—

Tythe-twined, established, dominant ? "In our ashes

    Still live our wonted fires." You could not brook,

        You said, "their fashes."

A perfect treasury of rustic lore

    You were to me, Old John : how nature thrives,

In horse or cow, their points, if less or more

    Convex the grunter's spine, the cackling wives

---

[1] Marked with the Cushag (ragwort).

Of Chanticleer how marked, the bird that dives,
And he that gobbles reddening—all the crises
　　You told, and ventures of their simple lives,
　　　　Also their prices.

The matchless tales your own great Wizard penned
　　To us were patent when you gave the key:
I knew Montrose; stern Clavers was my friend:
　　I carved the tombs with Old Mortality;
　　I sailed with Hatterick on the stormy sea:
Curled Cavalier, and Roundhead atrabiliar,
　　The shifts of Caleb Balderstone, to me
　　　　Were quite familiar.

But most of all, where all was most, I liked
　　To hear the story of the martyrs' doom;
The camp remote by stubborn hands bedyked;
　　The bones that bleached amid the heather bloom,
　　The gray haired sire; the intrepid maid for whom
Old Solway piled his waters monumental,
　　And gave that glorious heart a glorious tomb
　　　　Worth Scotia's rental.

Old John, such stories were to me a proof

      That 'neath the dimpling of the temporal tides

A power is working still in our behoof,

      A primal power that in the world abides.

      In virgins' hearts it lives, and tender brides

Confess it.   Veil your crests, ye powers of evil!

      It is an older power, and it derides

               Your vain upheaval.

Old John, do you remember Injebreck,

      And that fine day we went to get a load

Of perfumed larch?   From many a ruddy fleck

      The resin oozed and dropped upon the road;

      And ever as we trudged you taught the code

Traditional of woodcraft.   Night came sparkling

      With all her gems, and devious to Tromode

               The stream ran darkling.

But we the westward height laborious clomb;

      Then from Mount Rule descended on the Strang,

And saw afar the pleasant lights of home,

      Whereat your cheering speech—" We'll na be lang ":

Also a wondrous chirp of eld you sang,
Till, when we came to Braddan Bridge, the clinging
    Of that inveterate awe enforced a pang
        That stopped the singing.

Yet when we gained the vantage of the hill,
    And breathed more freely on the gentler slope,
Then quickly we recovered, as men will ;
    For Life's sweet buoyancy with Death can cope,
    Being strung by Nature for that genial scope :
And so, when you had ceased from your dejection,
    You talked with me of God, and faith, and hope,
        And resurrection.

'Twas thus I learned to love the various man,
    Rich patterned, woven of all generous dyes,
Like to the tartan of some noble clan,
    Blending the colours that alternate rise.
    So ever 'tis refreshing to mine eyes
To look beyond convention's flimsy trammell,
    And ee the native tints, in anywise,
        Of God's enamel.

Old John, you were not of the Calvinists ;

    "The doctrine o' yElaction," you declared—

You gentlest of all gentle Methodists—

    "A sawl-destroying doctrine." Whoso dared

    God's mercy limit he must be prepared

For something awful, not propounded clearly,

But dark as deepest doom that Dante bared,

             Or very nearly.

On Sunday morning early to the "class,"

    Then Matins, as it's called in ritual puff

Correct, then Evensong—but let that pass ;

    Our curate frowns. Nor then had you enough ;

    But, with your waistcoat pocket full of snuff,

You scorned the flesh, suppressed the stomach's clamour,

    And went where you could get "the real stuff"

             Absolved from grammar.

And who shall blame you, John ? Our prayers are good—

    Compact of precious fragments, passion-clips

Of many souls, cemented with the blood

    Of suffering. So we kiss them with the lips

Of awful love; but when the irregular grips

Of zeal constrain the cleric breast or laic,

    Into a thousand fiery shreds it rips

          Our old mosaic.

And so it was with you, Old John: the form

    Was excellent; but you were timely nursed

Upon a Cameronian lap, the storm

    Of that great strife inherited: the thirst

    For God was in you from the very first;

The rushing flood, the energy ecstatic,

    O'erwhelmed you that you could not choose but burst

          All bonds prelatic.

No gentler soul e'er took its earthward flight

    From Heaven's high towers, or clove the ethereal blue

With softer wings, or full of purer light

    Sweet Saint Theresa, bathed in virgin dew,

    Your sister was; but Jenny Geddes was too.

The false Archbishop feared the accents surly

    Of your firm voice you were John Knox, and you

          Balfour of Burley.

Then is it wonderful in me you found

     Disciple apt for every changing mood?

I also had a root in Scottish ground.

     No tale of ancient wrong my spirit wooed

     In vain : I loved the splendid fortitude,

Although we served in different battalions—

     Your folk were Presbyterians, mine were lewd

          Episcopalians.

What joy it was to you the day I came

     To visit that dear home, no longer mine !

I sat belated, having seen the flame

     Of sunset flash from well-known windows.   Nine

     Was struck upon the clock, and yet no sign

Of my departure ; then some admiration

     Of what I purposed ; then I could divine

          A consultation.

That I should sleep with you was their intent,

     And so we slept, being comrades old and tried.

It was to me a very sacrament,

     As you lay hushed and reverent at my side.

Your comely portance filled my soul with pride
To think how human dignity surpasses
    The estimate of those who " can't abide
             The lower classes."

And, severed by a curtain on a string,
    Slept Robert, and his wife, your daughter, slept ;
Slept little Beenie, and the bright-eyed thing
    You Maggie called, she to her mother crept
    And snuggled in the dark.   The night wind swept
" Aboon the thatch " ; came dawn, and touched each rafter
    With tongue of gold ; then from the bed I leapt
         As light as laughter.

But I must " break my fast " before I went :
    And so I sat, and shared the pleasant meal :
And all were up, and happy, and content :
    And last you prayed.   May Fashion ne'er repeal
    That self respect, those manners pure and leal !
My countrymen, I charge you never stain them ;
    But, as you love your Island's noblest weal,
         Guard and maintain them.

O faithfullest ! my debt to you is long:

    Life's grave complexity around me grows.

From you it comes if in the busy throng

    Some friends I have, and have not any foes ;

    And even now, when purple morning glows,

And I am on the hills, a night-worn watchman,

    I see you in the centre of the rose,

            Dear, brave, old Scotchman !

CHALSE A KILLEY

To Chalse in Heaven

So you are gone, dear Chalse!
    Ah, well; it was enough
    The ways were cold, the ways were rough
    Oh Heaven! oh home!
    No more to roam
        Chalse, poor Chalse.

And now it's all so plain, dear Chalse '
    So plain
    The wildered brain,
    The joy, the pain
The phantom shapes that haunted.

The half-born thoughts that daunted—

    All, all is plain

      Dear Chalse !

  All is plain.

  Yet where you're now, dear Chalse

    Have you no memory

    Of land and sea,

    Of vagrant liberty—

  Through all your dreams

  Come there no gleams

  Of morning sweet and cool,

  On old Barrule—

Breathes there no breath,

Far o'er the hills of Death,

  Of a soft wind that dallies

  Among the Curragh sallies—

Shaking the perfumed gold-dust on the streams ?

    Chalse, poor Chalse !

Or, is it all forgotten, Chalse ?

  A fever fit that vanished with the night—

  Has God's great light

    C

Pierced through the veiled delusions,
The errors and confusions ;
    And pointed to the tablet, where
      In quaint and wayward character,
As of some alien clime,
His name was graven all the time?
        All the time !
        O Chalse ! poor Chalse.

Such music as you made, dear Chalse !
    With that crazed instrument
That God had given you here for use-
You will not wonder now if it did loose
    Our childish laughter, being writhen and bent
    From native function—was it not, sweet saint?
But when such music ceases,
'Tis God that takes to pieces
    The inveterate complication
    And makes a restoration,
    Most subtle in its sweetness,
    Most strong in its completeness,
    Most constant in its meetness ;

And gives the absolute tone,

    And so appoints your station

Before the throne—

        Chalse, poor Chalse.

And yet while you were here, dear Chalse !

    You surely had more joy than sorrow :

    Even from your weakness you did borrow

A strength to mock

The frowns of fortune, to decline the shock

    Of rigorous circumstance,

    To weave around your path a dance

Of "airy nothings," Chalse ; and while your soul,

    Dear Chalse ! was dark

As an o'erwaned moon from pole to pole,

    Yet had you still an arc

    Forlorn, a silvery rim

    Of the same light wherein the cherubim

Bathe their glad brows, and veer

On circling wings above the starry sphere—

        Chalse, poor Chalse.

Yes, you had joys, dear Chalse! as when forsooth,

Right valiant for the truth,

　　You crossed the Baldwin hills,

　　And at the Union Mills,

Inspired with sacred fury,

You helped good Parson Drury

　　To "put the *Romans* out,"

　　A champion brave and stout

Ah now, dear Chalse! of all the radiant host,

Who loves you most?

　　　I think I know him, kneeling on his knees--

　　　Is it Saint Francis of Assise?

　　　　Chalse, poor Chalse.

Great joy was yours, dear Chalse! when first I met you

　　　In that old Vicarage

That shelters under Bradda : we did get you

　　By stratagem most sage

Of youthful mischief- got you all unweeting

　　Of mirthful toys,

　　A merry group of girls and boys,

To hold a missionary meeting

　　And you did stand upon a chair,

In the best parlour there ;
And dear old Parson Corrin was from home,
And I did play a tune upon a comb ;
 And unto us
 You did pronounce a speech most marvellous,
Dear Chalse ! and then you said
And *sthrooghed* the head—
 "If there'll be no objection,
 We'll now *purseed* to the collection "—
  Chalse, poor Chalse.

And do you still remember, Chalse,
 How at the Dhoor— ˙
 Near Ramsey, *to be sure*—
I got two painters painting in the chapel
 To make with me a congregation ?
And you did mount the pulpit, and did grapple
 With a tremendous text, and warn the nation
 Of drunkenness ; and in your hand
Did wave an empty bottle, so that we,
By palpable typology,
 Might understand—

CHALSE A KILLEY

Dear Chalse, you never had
An audience more silent or more sad.

And have you met him, Chalse,
Whom you did long to meet?
You used to call him *dear and sweet*—
Good Bishop Wilson—has he *taken you
In hand*, dear Chalse; and is he true,
And is he kind,
And do you tell him all your mind,
Dear Chalse,
All your mind?
And have you yet set up the press;
And is the type in readiness,
Founded with gems
Of living sapphire dipped
In blood of molten rubies, diamond-tipped?
And, *with the sanction of the Governor*,
Do you, a proud compositor,
Stand forth, and *print the Hemns?*
Chalse, poor Chalse.

ABER STATIONS

STATIO PRIMA

WHY do I make so much of Aber fall?
Four years ago
My little boy was with me here—
That's all—
He died next year :
He died just seven years old,
A very gentle child, yet bold,
Having no fear.
You have seen such?
They are not much?
No . . . no.
And yet he was a very righteous child,
Stood up for what was right,
Intolerant of wrong—

Pure azure light

Was cisterned in his eyes ;

We thought him wise

Beyond his years—so sweet and mild,

But strong

For justice, doing what he could—

Poor little soul—to make all children good.

I almost think—and yet I am to blame—

He was a different child from others ;

He had three sisters and two brothers :

He seemed a little king

Among the children—ah ! 'tis a common thing—

Parents are all the same--

You've seen those kings—yes, yes—

Of course . . . and yet . . . the righteousness . . .

The . . . Never mind ! he came

With me to Aber fall

That's all, that's all.

STATIO SECUNDA

Just listen to the blackbird - what a note

The creature has ! God bless his happy throat !

He is so absolutely glad

I fear he will go mad.

Look here ! this very grit

I crush beneath my boot

His little foot

Trod crisp that day—

That's it ! that's it !

Oh what is there to say ?

The little foot so warm and pink !

Oh what is there to think ?

His mother kissed it every night

When she put out the light—

And where ?

What is it now ? a fascicle

Of crumbling bones

Jammed in with earth and stones.

You say that this is old,

A tale twice-told—

Say what you will,

Old, new, I swear

That it is horrible—

Horrible, blackbird, howsoe'er

The Spring rejoice you with its budding bloom—

Yes, horrible, most horrible!

Though you should carol to the crack of doom,

Poor blackbird! being so absolutely glad

I hope he won't go mad.

Statio Tertia

The stream is very sweet

To-day . . . Just see the swallow dart!

How fleet!

It sent a shiver to my heart.

If he had lived, you say -

Well, well—if he had lived, what then?

Some men

Will always argue—yes, I know . . . of course . .

The argument has force.

If he had lived, he might have changed-

From bad to worse?

Nay, my shrewd balance-setter,

Why not from good to better?

Why not to best? to joy

And splendour? oh my boy!

I did not want this argument in the least,

My soul had ceased

From doubt and questioning—

That swallow's wing !

What a transcendent rush !

Hush ! hush !

Or, if you talk, talk low :

For . . . do you know . . .

Just as the swallow dipt,

I felt as if a soft hand slipt

Its fingers into mine . . . he's near . . .

He's with us . . . 'tis not right the child should hear

This jangling . . . low then, low !

Or this is better . . . go,

Go, darling ; play upon the bank,

And prank

Your hair with daisy and with buttercup,

And we will meet you higher up.

Now then . . . *if he had lived?* if my sweet son

Had lived? . . . You stare . . .

There ! there !

"Tis gone, 'tis gone—

It was the swallow's dart

That sent a shiver to my heart.

STATIO QUARTA

We have not seen the sun for many days,
But now through East-wind haze
He makes a shift
To send a luminous drift,
To which, as to his full unclouded splendour
The meek, contented earth makes glad surrender.
God bless the simple earth
That gave me birth !
God bless her that she looks so pleased—
The soul that is diseased
With this world's sorrow—Well, sir ? ought to look ?
Beyond, and yet beyond: not in this narrow nook
Of His creation
Will God make up His book.
The whole is one great scheme
Of compensation—
The net result
Is all . . . I too have had my dream,
As from my nonage dedicate a μύστης
Of that great cult.

I saw lord Love upon his galley pass

Westward from Cyprus ; smooth as glass .

The sea was all before him.   He, as κελευστής,

Stood at the stern, and piped

The rhythms ; but, ever and anon,

As worked upon

By some familiar fury, grasping a scourge

(An amethyst

Fastened it to his wrist . . . Love's wrist !),

He ran along the transtra, and did urge

The rowers, and striped

Their backs with blood ; whereat they lept

Like maddened hounds, and swept

The sea until it hissed.

Then I—

"Lord Love, what means this cruelty ? "

But he to me

Deigned no reply :

Only I saw his face was wet with tears,

And he did look "beyond, and yet beyond : "

But those men fond

And fatuous never turned

Their eyes from his, but yearned

With an insensate yearning, having confidence

That so it must be : but on what pretence

I know not—Ah most cruel lord !

Ah knotted cord !

Dull plash

Of livid tissues ! flash

Of oars that smote the waters to a hum . . .

Come, come !

You've had enough of this –

But what I meant, and what you seemed to miss,

Was simply how the meek, contented earth,

That gave me birth,

Was pleased . . .

Then you of *soul diseased*,

And what not . . . excellent !

But that is what I meant.

STATIO QUINTA

The shepherd calls –

How these great mountain walls

Re echo ! See his dog

Come limping from the bog !

How far he holds him

With that thin clamour !   Scolds him ?

Or cheers him—which ?

Say both—most like.   The pitch

Is steep, poor fellow !

And still that bellow—

Ya, ya !

Whoop ! tittiva !

And Echo from her niche

Shrieks challenged.   Shout,

O shepherd ! flout

The irritable Echo till she raves !

As man behaves,

So God apportions, doing what is best

For you, and for the rest.

As man behaves ?   You do not help me much,

Nay, sir, nor touch

The central point at all—

Retributive, mechanical—

I see it.   But outside all this

I miss. . . I miss . . .

Sir, know you Death ?   Permit me introduce . . .

No ?   *What's the use ?*

The use ! . . . One thing I can collect,

You have but scant respect

For Death. Why, sir, he made a feint

That very minute at you—quaint !

The way he grins and skips—

Whips ! whips !

Down ! down ! good dog ! good Death !

To heel, you rogue !

Good Death ! good dog !

You'd rather not behold him ?

I've told him—

'I faith,

He'd frighten you, would Death.

Provoke me—yes, you did—

The shepherd chid

His lagging hound—

I had no other thought

But how mad Echo caught

The sound

Of that exasperant call,

And made it bound

Back from the mountain wall.

STATIO SEXTA

Ho! snow

Upon the crags!

How slow

The winter lags!

Ha, little lamb upon the crags,

How fearlessly you go!

Take care

Up there,

You little woolly atom!   On and on

He goes . . . 'tis steep . . . Hillo!

My friend is gone,

Friend orthodoxo-logical—

He could not argue with a waterfall!

And here it is—my Aber . . . Stay!

I'll cross

This way:

The moss

Upon these stones is dripping with the spray—

And now one turn, left hand,

And I shall stand

Before the very rock : not yet . . . not yet !

Oh let me think !   No, no !   I don't forget

(Forget !)—but this is sacred . . . peace then, peace !

Release

From all dead things, that serve not to present

At my soul's grate the lovely innocent.

He had heard some idle talk

Of how his father had great strength to walk

And climb ;

And so he thought that he must lose no time,

But instantly addressed

His little breast

To that tall cliff,

Smooth, perpendicular, too stiff

For cragsman from the wildest Hebrides,—

But he did bend his knees,

And spread his little arms, and laid

His body to the work, and made

Such genuine effort of ascent

As though he meant

To reach the top, of course, and had no doubt

Of what he was about—

So serious   no passing whim

Oh no ! *'Twas thus his father clomb*

And he had come

To climb like him.

And is he here?

O Braddan, are you here?

O darling, have no fear !

Speak to me ! breathe some fond thing in my ear !

But what should Braddan know

Of me, and what I am,

And what I want—the little lamb !

What should he know,

Who four brief years ago

Knew only what a little child should know !

Should some kind angel, who doth teach my child,

Some angel with the love-deep eyes,

Some angel charged to keep him undefiled,

Hear my sad cries,

And bring him unto me,

Is my whole heart a thing for him to see?

Am I prepared that his sweet honesty

Should search it through and through?

Oh eyes of honest blue !

Oh fearless eyes !

Oh mild surprise!

Oh is there one, one chamber of my heart

That's fit

For him to sit

Therein, till it is time to part?

Or could I come to him?

No matter where—

Swim,

Swim the dark river, and be there?

Could a deep acquiescence

Convey me to his presence?

And if it could,

What were it after all

But as a young prince stood

Upon the city wall,

And saw his foster-father at the gate,

And wondered at his mean estate,

And made no sign

Unto the warders? But my Braddan's mine!

Mine! mine! and none's beside!

O helpless men! has everything been tried?

Where does the secret hide?

Is it a simple thing perhaps?

Yea, after all, a very simple thing,

That through the lapse

Of all the ages any tide

Might bring,

Nay, every tide has brought

Up to the level of our thought?

Is the blest converse that I crave

The function of a faculty we have,

But know not how to use, being, by some dark mischance,

Time-prisoned in a rooted ignorance?

A faculty which, if no God forbad it,

An accident might bring to light,

And some one, somewhere, waking in the night,

Would know he had it.

But we are cumbered with our egotisms ;

A thousand prisms,

Hung round our souls, refract the single ray,

That else would show us instantly the way.

So even now, when my sad heart aspires

To height of paramount desires,

These verses mock it

With their rhyme-jangles, frustrate as a rocket,

That mounts, and breaks, and falls in coloured fading fires.

A curse

Upon the impotent verse !

Yet, no !

Not so—

It may be that in these

The soul shall yet win something more than ease ;

For song is of the essence, and, who sings,

Touches the central springs—

Ah vain imaginings !

Let be ! let be !

O Braddan, pity me !

Yes, yes !

I know there is another way — press, press.

And I will press, sweet Braddan.

Sink, thought ! sink, sink !

To think

Is but to madden.

Stop, heart !

You have no part

In this   die, soul,

Die, die ! it must be soon

The barrier's but a film ; one gasp, and I shall swoon

Into his arms

Braddan! why, Braddan! see, I keep my tryst—

O God! O Christ!

That snow

Is very slow

To disappear : how winter lags!

I see the dam

Upon the crags,

But nowhere can I see the little lamb.

STATIO SEPTIMA

The heavens are very blue

Above the western hill ;

The earth is very still—

I will draw near, and view

The spot

Where he is . . . not.

But O dear cliff, O big good-natured giant,

I think some delicate dint must still remain

On your broad surface, from the strain

Of limbs so sweetly pliant.

Behold!

The lamb! the lamb! fallen from the very rock!

Cold! cold!

Dead! dead!

His little head

Rests on the very block

That Braddan trod—

Dear lambs! twin lambs of God!

Old cliff, such things

Might move some stubborn questionings—

But now I question not—

See, see! the waterfall

Is robed in rainbows—what!

Our lambs?   My Braddan shall have charge

Of him, and lead him by the marge

Of some bright stream celestial.

Braddan shall be a happy shepherd boy;

No trouble shall annoy

That soft green pasture   Ah, Murillo, saint!

Kind friend! that for all sorrowing hearts did'st paint

John Baptist and the Lamb—those arms thrown round

That neck!   Forgive me, God, that I have found

Some comfort in this little parable

It gives me strength to climb the hill,

And humbly so return -

God bless the merry burn !

I have no will

But thine, O God !   I know that Thou art true—

Be blue, O heavens, be blue !

Be still, O earth, be still !

LLANFAIRFECHAN,
  April 17, 1879.

EPISTOLA AD DAKYNS

Dakyns, when I am dead,
Three places must by you be visited,
Three places excellent,
Where you may ponder what I meant,
And then pass on
Three places you must visit when I'm gone.

Yes, *meant*, not *did*, old friend!
For neither you nor I shall see the end,
And do the thing we wanted:
Natheless three places will be haunted
By what of me
The earth and air
Shall spare,

And fire and sea

Let be—

Three places only,

Three places, Dakyns.

I

The first is by the Avon's side,

Where tall rocks flank the winding tide.

There come when morning's virgin kiss

Awakes from dreams the clematis,

And every thorn and briar is set

As with a diamond coronet—

There come, and pause upon the edge,

And I will lean in every ledge,

And melt in grays, and flash in whites,

And linger in a thousand lights ;

And yield in bays, and urge in capes,

And fill the old familiar shapes ;

And yearn in curves, and strain to meet

The pensive pressure of your feet.

And you shall feel an inner sense,

A being kindred and intense ;

And you shall feel a strict control,

A something drawing at your soul,

A going out, a life suspended,

A spirit with a spirit blended.

And you shall start as from a dream,

While I, withdrawing down the stream,

Drift vaporous to the ancient sea,

A wraith, a film, a memory

Three places, Dakyns.

II

The next is where a hundred fells

Stand round the Lake like sentinels,

Where Derwent, like a sleeping beauty,

Girdled with that watchful duty,

At Skiddaw's foot securely lies,

And gives her bosom to the skies.

O come ! and I will bid the moon

All subtle harmonies attune

That live in shadows and in heights,

A mystic chorus of delights.

O come where many an island bevels

Its strand to meet the golden levels!

O lay your heart upon each line,

So diamond-cut and crystalline,

That seams the marble of the mere,

And smoothes all trouble, calms all fear,

With that sweet natural straightness, free

From effort or inconstancy.

O draw your thought with all its passion

Along the melancholy fashion

Of forms accentuate with the beat

Of the great Master's rhythmic feet.

But when upon the finest verge

The sense no further flight can urge,

When the full orb of contemplation

Is stretched, a nameless tribulation

Shall sway the whole, a silent stress

Borne in upon that loveliness;

A burden as of human ills,

A human trouble in the hills;

A quickening pulse in earth and sky,

And you shall know that it is I—

Three places, Dakyns.

III

The next is where God keeps for me
A little island in the sea,
A body for my needs, that so
I may not all unclothed go,
A vital instrument whereby
I still may commune with the sky,
When death has loosed the plaited strands,
And left me feeling for the lands.
Even now between its simple poles
It has the soul of all my souls.
But then   whatever I have been,
Whatever felt, whatever seen,
Whatever guessed, or understood,
The tones of right, the tints of good,
The loves, the hates, the hopes, the fears,
The gathered strength of all my years—
All that my life has in me wrought
Of complex essence shall be brought
And wedded to those primal forms
That have their scope in calms and storms,

Attuned to the swells and falls

Of Nature's holy intervals.

And, old coeval use surviving,

No need shall be for any striving,

No need from point to point to press,

And swell the growing consciousness,

But in a moment I shall sit

Sphered in the very heart of it.

And every hill from me shall shoot,

And spread as from a central root,

And every crag and every spur

To me its attitude refer :

And I shall be the living heart,

And I shall live in every part,

With elemental cares engrossed,

And all the passion of the coast.

Come then, true Dakyns, be the test

Most meet to make me manifest !

Come, and immediate recognise

To all your moods the dumb replies.

Or stretch across a kindly void

The golden life-chords unalloyed

With thought, and instant they shall make

The music they were made to make.
Thus shall you grow into a sense
Of islandhood, not taking thence
Some pretty surfaces and angles,
Tricking your soul, as with fine spangles
A savage studs his wampum belt.
But patient till the whole is felt,
And you become incorporate
Into an undivided state.
Then shall your body be as dead :
And you shall take to you instead
The system of the natural powers,
The heath that blooms, the cloud that lowers,
The antithesis of things that bide,
The cliff, the beach, the rock, the tide
The lordly things, whose generous feud
Is but a fixed vicissitude.
Wherefore, O Maughold, if he come,
If Dakyns come,
Let not a voice be dumb
In any cave ;
Fling up the wave
In wreaths of giddy spray :

O'er all the bay

Flame out in gorse around the "kern," [1]

And let his heart within him burn,

Until he gains the slope

Where, in the "sure and certain hope,"

Sleep the long rows :

Then let him quench the fiery gleams

In Death's gray shadow of repose,

As one who dreams

He knows not what, and yet he knows

I have her there

That was a bud so rare.

But, Bradda, if he come to you,

I charge you to be true !

Sit not all sullen by the sea,

But show that you are conscious it is he.

It is no vulgar tread

That bends the heath :

Broad be the heavens spread

Above, the sea beneath

Blue with *that* blue !

And let the whispering airs

---

[1] Cairn.

E

Move in the ferns.   By those strong prayers

Which rent my heart that day as lightning rends a cloud,

And rips it till it glares

To open view : by all the vows I vowed,

I charge you, and I charge you by the tears

And by the passion that I took

From you, and flung them to the vale,

And had the ultimate vision, do not fail !

Three places only —

Three places, Dakyns.

CLIFTON, *December* 1869.

IN THE COACH

No. I.—JUS' THE SHY

YES, comin home from the North Sea fishin we were, past
    John o' Grotes,

Past the Pentlands and Cape Wrath theer, twenty boats

There'd be of us, and eight men and boys to every one, and
    how many are you makin that?

A hunderd-and-sixty, says you—You're smart though, what?

And sure enough it is—aw this ciphrin and figgurin and
    recknin, aw grand! grand!

Well, when we hauled to the Southward, the wind turned a
    foul, you'll understand;

So we made for a bay though, the lot of us: terble narra it
    was to get in—

That bay—but spreadin out astonishin,

And the room you navar seen—acres! acres!   So swings to
    an anchor for all

As aisy as aisy, and plenty to spare, just that we could call

The time o' day and that: it's comfible, you know, like
    yandhar, and mayve a matthar

Of ten fathom— good houldin, fuss-rate ridin, couldn be
    batthar.

And at the top of the bay there was a castle, terble though,

Aw bless ye, terble uncommon, and the gardens theer all
    in a row,

And all above one another; and some guns that was took
    from the Rooshians, and a tower, and a flag goin
    a-haulin—

I don' know the burgee, but as broad as a good tarpaulin:

And over the door, cut to a dot, aw open your eyes the
    widest you can!

Over the door, if you plaze, over the door, what next?
    God bless us! the three legs of Man!

That was the thing.   My gough! the wondher we had:

And this and that: but at last Billy Fargher said

It muss ha' been some of these ould Earls or Dukes, or
    their daughters, or their nieces, or their cousins

(Of coorse, th're'd be dozens)

That got married on yandhar lek—

At laste you'd expeck

There'd be some workin in and out ; and blood is blood,

That's aisy understood,

And navar ashamed of the ould flag, not her, but heisin it
to the wind, and carvin it on the stone, like defyin,

Lek as bould as a lion.

Now there was a terble great lady livin in this Castle, mind!

Aye, a lady, bless ye ! and no mistake, grand, no doubt, but
kind.

And she come to see us, aye, and she said she was once on
the Islan',

*And the people was that good to her, and that civil, and that
smilin,*

And that plazzant, she said, *that she couldn forget it,* she
said,

No, she said ; *and it wasn no use,* she said,

They were nice people, she said, *the nice you couldn tell ;*

That's what she said, and she liked them well.

And she wouldn take no res' of us but we muss promise
then and theer

To have dinner with her, aye ! dinner, think of that now !
a hundred-and-sixty of us—what ? aw I'll sweer.

Dinner though ; so promised sure enough ; and the day come,

And there wasn a sowl of us went, not a sowl, by gum !

No ! and the pipers blawin,

And the curks drawin,

And the preparation they'd be havin, so I'm toul',

And there wasn a sowl, no, not a sowl.

And what for was that ? What for ? just the shy, the shy,

That's the what for, and that's the why,

And that's the way with the Manx ; aw, it is though, aw,
　　　they are, they are,

Mos' despard shy ; aw it's a pity for all, but star'

They will, and wink and nudge and poke and bother,

And spit theer and laugh, and look like axin one another

"Are you goin, and you ?" and takin rises, and all to that,

Till you can't tell is it your granny's cat

Or what is it that's doin on you, but you feel jus' a reglar
　　　fool,

And all the time hitendin to be as cool as cool.

Aw dear ! it's a pity ! a pity ! aw a rum lot !

But, whether or not,

The great lady was agate of us again,

Deed for sure she was, and she seen the men

Was hy of the dinner ; but it's lek she thought

It was on account of not knowin how to behave theerselves

    the way they ought

With theer knives and theer plates and the lek ; so axed

    them to tay—

Aw she muss ha' been a kind lady anyway.

And we promised faithful, and the day come, and she sent

    and she sent,

And there wasn a one of us went.

The shy, did ye say ?   Sartinly, nothin but the shy,

That's the way we are ; aye,

Treminjus though.   I was raelly sorry for her, I was, I tell

    ye,

And all the throuble that was at her theer, fit for a melya,

And the disappointed—what? and, altogather, my chiarn !

These Manx chaps isn fit, no they arn'—

Terble boghs !

  Well the wind veered round, and we all sailed for the

    Southward,

Excep' two boats.   Now, d'ye think she'd ha' bothered

About such dunkies ?   Well, that's jus' what she did,

Perseverin, aye ! and considherin, and waitin.   "Turn your

    quid ! "

Says Juan Jem, lek *futhee*, lek *no hurry !* you know

Lek *aisy all!* lek *keep her so!*

Lek *wait and see!*   Patient, is it?   But anyway the strong

The kindness was in her—that's it, and the long-

Suffrin lek, and navar not no capers of takin offince.

My gough! it's many a time I've thought of it since.

What did she do but down to these chaps that was lavin

      behind

Sixteen of them, aye— and axed them theer as kind as kind—

To tay? most sartin; what else? and I tell ye they took

      heart and went.

And enjoyed theerselves to the full the same's it might be

      you or any other gent,

But the res' l you're wondrin.   Chut!

Jus' the shy, and nothin *but*

The shy.   Aw, no use a' talkin,

The shy it's shawkin.

No raison, says you: not a bit.

Amazin, says you.   Well, that's all you'll get,

That is the raison, and the for and the why

Jus' the shy.

No. II.· Yes, ma'am! no, ma'am!

Yes, ma'am, no, ma'am :

We called him Joe, ma'am ;

Eighteen—

My name's Cregeen—

Yes, ma'am, no, ma'am ;

Had to go, ma'am.

Faver ? aye ;

Young to die ;

Eighteen for spring.

(*Chorus of sympathisers*) " Poor thing ! poor thing ! "

Yes, ma'am, no, ma'am ;

I'm rather low, ma'am—

Bombay—

Not at say.

Yes, ma'am, no, ma'am ;

Just so, ma'am,

Clane groun',

And the Pazon in his gown ;

No stone, just marks.

(*Chorus as before*) " She's thinkin of these sharks."

Yes, ma'am, no, ma'am,

Not like home, ma'am

The clothes he died in

The corp was plied in.

Yes, ma'am, no, ma'am ;

But just to sew, ma'am,

Something sof',

Plazed enough,

But couldn be—

(*Chorus as before*) " My chree ! my chree ! "

Yes, ma'am, no, ma'am,

We were callin him Joe, ma'am

His chiss come,

Not like to some ;

Yes, ma'am, no, ma'am,

Come by Crow, ma'am,

From Liverpool :

And, of a rule,

Not amiss.

(*Chorus as before*) "She's got his chiss ! she's got his

chiss "

Yes, ma'am, no, ma'am,

These feer'ns [1] will grow, ma'am,

So I'm tould.

But I'm makin very bould.

Yes, ma'am, no, ma'am—

Rather slow, ma'am,

Is this coach ;

But I hope I don't encroach—

In my head the pain 's.

(*Chorus as before*) "In her heart she manes."

Yes, ma'am, no, ma'am.

No. III.—CONJERGAL RIGHTS

Conjergal rights ! conjergal rights !

I don't care for the jink of her and I don't care for the jaw
    of her,

But I'll have the law of her.

Conjergal rights ! yis, yis, I know what I'm sayin

Fuss-rate, Misthress Corkhill, fuss-rate, Misther Cain,

And all the people in the coach—is there a man or a
    woman of the lot of ye—

[1] Ferns.

Well now, that's what I wudn have thought of ye,

I wudn raelly   No, I *haven' got a little sup*,

Not me   is there one of ye that wudn stand up

For conjergal rights?

No, ma'am, *tight 's*

Not the word, not a drop since yesterday.   But lizzen, good
     people, lizzen !

I'll have her in the coorts, I'll have her in prison—

It's the most scandalous thing you ever—What ! this woman
     and her daughter—

It's clane murder, it's abslit manslaughter,

Aye, and I wudn trus' but beggamy, that's what it is-
     married yesterday mornin

In Kirk Breddhan Church, and not the smallest taste of warnin,

Takes her to her house in Castletown,

And jus' for I axed a quashtin -and I'll be boun'

It's a quashtin any one of you wud have axed—picks a
     quarrel, makes a row,

The two of them, aye, the two of them bow wow !

Hammer and tungs ! sends for a pleeceman, puts me to the
     door

But I'll owe her ! I'll owe her !

Aisy, Mr. Cretney ?   No, I'll not be aisy ;

It's enough to make a body crazy,

That's what it is, and the supper on the table,

And the hoss in' the stable.

And I said nothin, nor I done nothin. Aw, if there's law
    in the land,

Law or justice, I'll have it, d'ye understand?

Do ye see the thing? My grayshurs! married is married,

Isn it? what? and me that carried

The woman's box. And that isn all; what raison? what
    sense?

Think of the expense! think of the expense!

Don't ye know? God bless me! The certif'cake, that's
    hafe-a-crown,

And the licence, that's five shillin, money down, money
    down!

And not a farlin off for cash, these Pazons, not a farlin;

And said she was my darlin

And all to that, guy heng! it's thrue! it's thrue!

And look at me now! boo-hoo-oo-oo!

Yis, cryin I am, and no wondher—

You don't see me it's that dark in the coach. By the livin
    thundher

I'm kilt mos'ly, that's what I am, almos' kilt

With throuble and disthress and all. *A jilt*,

You say, *a jilt!* But married, married, married, d'ye hear?

Married, Misthress Creer,

Married afore twelve at Kirk Breddhan,

Married, a reglar proper weddin

And no mistake,

And this woman . . . O my gough! don't spake of her!
don't spake!

It's me that's spakin? Yis, and I will! I will!

Who's to spake if I amn'? But still —

It's lek you don't see the coach is so dark, and no light from
these houses,

But feel of this new coat, and the pair of new trousis,

Bought o' puppose, o' puppose! what else?

Bran new; and the shirt and the frells,

And the cuffs and the collar, every d —— thing

As bran and as new as a gull's wing -

And all to plaze her, and to look accordin

To the occasion, and to do her credit, and ho'rdin

The teens of months. And oh if I'd only borrowed them
from a neighbour,

That's the thing, but bought them, bought them; and even
so they might ha' been chaber,

Yis, they might, at another shop. But you don' see the
    way I'm goin,

No, no, you don'—

But I'd lek you to—the tears! I'm jus' slushin the sthraw

With the tears, making the coach all damp for the people—
    yis, I know I am, but I'll have the law, I'll have the
    law.

Just a quashtin about a bit of proppity,

The house, in fac', the very house we come into, d'ye see?

The house, her house! of coorse! of coorse! But goodness
    grayshurs!

Who doesn know the law about a thing like that? the
    iggorant! the ordashurs!

If ever there was a thing on God's earth

That was mine, it was yandhar house! But it isn worth

Talkin—no! There's people that'll go against anything.
    But what! no suttlement goin a-makin

Nor nothin, jus' everything goin a-takin

Undher the common law of matrimony theer—

At my massy! at my massy! with your lave, Mr. Tear,

At my massy, sir. You'll scuse me.

But you know the law. Married—my chree! my chree!

What *iss* " married," if that isn? it's as plain as a dus'bin—

Your own dear lovin husbin

As kind as kind !

See the beauty of it ! And "all that's thine is mine,"

Isn it sayin that in the Bible?

And surely the woman is li'ble

As well as the man ; and to "love, honour, and obey,"

Isn that what they say?

But it's my heart, that's it ! my poor broken heart ! aw
     dear ! aw dear !

And my feelins ! my feelins ! and that son of mine girnin
     from ear to ear,

And his lip and his imprince, and his disrespeck,

And the waste and the neglec'—

Oh it's awful ! it's awful ! oh the wounds that there's no
     healins !

Oh my feelins ! my feelins !

But I'll see aburt, I will, I'll see aburt

The dirt !

The wife of my bosom ! Don't be mockin '

I heard a woman laughin : its shockin'

That a woman 'd laugh at the lek of such doins, yis, it is,

Downright wickedness

A woman that I could name

Fic for shame ! fic for shame !

But I'll have law.   Look here ! is James Gell a lawyer?
>   You'll hardly uphould me

He isn, will ye ? James Gell—the Attorney-Gineral : well,
>   that's the man that tould me.

Did I spake to him about it ? was I axin him afore

I was anything to her ?

Sartinly ! my gough ! was I goin to run my neck into a noose

And navar no 'pinion nor . . . I'm not such a goose

As yandhar ither, I've gorrit in writin, yis, I have,

I've gorrit here—aw, you'll get lave ! you'll get lave !

Not aisy to read, but God bless me ! where's my specs ?
>   But lar't ! lar't

It's my feelins : O my heart ! my heart !

My poor heart ! my poor heart ! boo-hoo-oo-oo !   Aye, and
>   you'd think there'd be

Some semperthy,

Some . . . Crow, open this door and let me out ! there's
>   no regard with ye

For a man's . . . I'll not ride another yard with ye . . .

Theer then ! theer ! No, I'll have none of your good-
>   nights . . .

Conjergal rights ! conjergal rights !

F

No. IV.—Going to meet him

A. Yes, yes, I'll be seein him, seein Billy

This very night—aw, I'm almost silly

With the thought. Yes, Mrs. Quayle, just a year away,

And he's comin home this very day.

Billy! Billy! aw the foolish I am!

And you'll 'scuse me, ladies, won't ye now? Aw, I'll be as
    qui't as a lamb,

Yes, I will : and it isn right

To be carryin on like this afore people, but aw the delight!

Oh I wonder how he'll be lookin ; he's that handsome and
    gud,

Aw, yes, aw dear ! I wud, I wud,

I wud flie, I wud die ! oh the darling ! oh it's shockin,

And I can't keep qui't, no, I can't, no, I can't, and it's no use
    o' talkin.

But I'll try, Mrs. Quayle, you know me : yes, I'll try, I'll do
    my best,

Oh I will though, and only proper lek. But how'l he be
    drest ?

O Billy, Billy ! will he have his white ducks ? ho, ho !

It's me that 'd make them like the driven snow ;

But these Liverpool washerwomen—chut! the nasty things!

    aw, I'll be bail

No notion whatever, no, they haven' ; what did ye say, Mrs.

    Quayle ?

Not to be expectin too much and I'll not be disappointed? and

    I'd batthar—

What, Mrs. Quayle, *batthar* what, what ? what ? I've got the

    latthar !

He's comin ! he's comin ! "On the spree," did ye say ?

Like the way

With such, Mrs. Quayle ? With such !

Mrs. Quayle ! Mrs. Quayle ! Who then ? whuch ?

This coach is chokin me, give me air—

No, no ! it isn fair,

Navar ! no, navar ! navar !

No, no ! you're clavar,

You've seen a dale,

Mrs. Quayle,

A dale, no doubt, but that you'll navar see,

For I love Billy, and Billy loves me !

Is that plain ? don't you know that ? It cudn ! it cudn !

But ye come upon me that sudden.

No, no! that's not Billy nor natur nor nothin; that's
    foolishness—

But I can't rest—

This coach is close—the hot I am and the coul'!

(*Chorus of conscious women*) Poor sowl! poor sowl!

B. Now then, now then, what do you say now?

Here he is, and I think you'll allow,

Eh, Mrs. Quayle, you'll allow, I think,

Not the smallest signs of drink.

And I ast your pardon humble I do

I'm forgettin myself.   But is it you?

Is it you? is it you?   Whisper then,

The millish ven!

Close, Billy, close—

God knows

I love you, Billy, and you love me,

Don't you, Billy? my chree! my chree!

Aw just to hear—

Chut! I'm foolish, but oh the dear!

The   *Steady*, did ye say? yis, Billy, yis!

Steady it is.

Now, Mrs. Quayle, is he drunk or sober?

Poor ould Billy! and last October

He sailed, poor chap! And *it's me that's drunk*—

With joy you mane? And have you got your trunk—

What am I talkin? your chiss—dear me! and didn I
    see't

Comin along the street—

Of coorse, and mended—

You tould me. Oh isn all this beautiful? isn it
    splendid?

Closer, Billy, closer then!

Crid shen?

Nothin, but . . . lizzen, Billy, whisp'rin's free

I love Billy, and he loves me . . .

Do you, Billy? as God's above

Do you love

Me, Billy? The word, Billy, as soft as soft—

What am I thinkin of?

Aw ye said it, ye said it. And now I'll trouble ye

Is he drunk or sober, this young man, W.

Sayle, by name? Aw you'll 'scuse me, won't ye?

Aw I didn mane to 'front ye,

Aw nothin of the surt; only ye see the glad

I am it's fit to drive me mad.

And I'm rather young . . . at laste, not that oul',

You'll 'scuse me, won't ye . . .

(*Chorus of conscious women*) Poor sowl! poor sowl!

No. V.--The Pazons

What's the gud of these Pazons? They're the most despard
  rubbage goin,

Reglar humbugs they are. Show me a Pazon, show me a
  drone!

Livin on the fat of the land, livin on the people's money

The same 's the drones is livin on the beeses honey.

Aw bless ye! the use of them? not the smallest taste in
  the world, no!

Grindin down the honest workin man, just so;

Suckin the blood of the poor and needy,

And as greedy's greedy.

See the tithes, see the fees, see the glebes and all;

What's the call

For the lek? and their wives go'n a takin for ladies, and
  their childhar go'n sendin to College

Like the fuss of the land.   Aw, it bates all knowledge

The uprisement of the lek.   And fingerin with their piannas,

Them that shud be singin their hosannahs

To the King of glory constant.   Clap them in the pulfit
    theer,

What can they do!   Aw come down the steer! come down
    the steer,

And don't be disgracin yourself that way.   That's what
    I've been thinkin many a time :

And let a praecher take his turn, a local, aye, just try 'm!

Aw give your people a chance to get salvation.

"Blow ye the trumpet in Zion!"   That's the style, and the
    prespiration

Pourin out all over his body!   See the wrestlin,

And the poor Pazon with his collec' and his pestlin

And his gosp'lin.   *Gospel!*   Let it sound abroad,

The rael gospel of God !

Aw then the happy I am !

Give us the Lamb ! give us the Lamb !

But he can't, I tell ye, he can't—

What's that young man sayin theer—rant ?

Rant indeed, is that what he's learnin

At Oxfoot College, to revile the spirit that's burnin

In the hearts of the faithful? Aye, and let it burn, let it
    blaze !

But here's the Pazon, if ye plaze,

Cocked up with his little twinkle of a farlin rush,

And 'll hauk and blush,

And his snips and his snaps

And his scrips and his scraps,

And endin up with the Lord's Prayer quite sudden

Like the ould woman's sauce to give a notion of a puddin,

Aye, puddin, and drabbin with their swishups and dishups

Of the stale ould broth of the law. If all the hands of
    all the bishops

Was goin crookin over his head, he wudn be a praecher,

Not him, *nor* a taecher.

You can't be married without a Pazon? Can't I though?

Can't I, Masther Crow?

Give me the chance: I'm a married man with a fam'ly
    comin,

But if it plazed the Lord to take Mrs. Creer, d'ye think
    there's a woman

d refuse to go with me before the High Bailiff down

At Castletown,

And ger' a slick of matrimony put upon us?

Honest?

Yes, honest thallure: *but holy, "holy matrimony," they're
say'n:*

Holy your grandmother!—at laste, I mane,

And astin your pardon, Mrs. Clague.

But the idikkilis people is about the lek o' yandhar—Aisy
with your leg,

Masthar Callow; thank ye! that'll do—

Yis, Mrs. Clague, and crizzenins and funarls too –

Shuperstition, just shuperstition, the whole kit,

Most horrid, just popery, clane popery, that's it—

Aye, popery and schamin and a lie and a delusion and
snares

To get money out of the people, which is the Lord's and
not theirs.

Money money every turn,

Money money—pay or burn!

And where does it come from? I said it before and I say
it again,

Out of the sweat of the workin man,

Aw these priests! these priests! these priests—

Down with them, I say. The brute beasts

Has more sense till us, that's willin to pay blackmail

To a set of rascals, to a pack of   Good evenin, Pazon
        Gale !

Good evenin, sir, good evenin !   Step up, sir ! make room,

Make room for our respected Vicar—and may I persume

To ax how is Mrs. Gale, sir, and the family ;

Does this weather agree—

Rather damp, I dessay.   And the Governor's got knighted ?

I'm delighted to see you, sir, delighted, delighted !

No. VI.   Noah's Ark

(*On the road*)

"Good gracious ! what in the world is this ?"—"A lil
        cauf, ma'am."

"Why, you don't mean to say . . . . ?"—"I'll take it by the
        scruff, ma'am ;

We'll just lave it at the door.

It's belongin to Mr. Moore.

"And to think the abominable brute

Was suckin at my boot !

Mr. Crow ! Mr. Crow !

I'd have you to know

"Jus a lil cauf, ma'am

Jus' a lil cauf."

(Arrival at Ramsey)

" Mercy on us ! what next ? "—" A lil dunkey, ma'am."

"A little what? Good heavens!"—"Aw, ye needn be
    funky, ma'am ;

I'll get him out as qui't . . .

Good people, bring a light !"

" But a solitary female in the dark. . .

With half the beasts in Noah's ark.

Mr. Crow ! Mr. Crow !

I'd have you to know . . ."

"Jus' a lil dunkey, ma'am

Jus' a lil dunkey."

GOB-NY-USHTEY

(Water's Mouth)

I saw a little stream to-day
That sprang right away
From the cornice of rock·
Sprang like a deer, not slid ;
And the Tritons to mock ─
Old dissolute Tritons—" Hurroo ! "
They said, "We'll teach him a thing or two,
This upland babe."   And I've no doubt they did.
But, as he lightly fell, midway
His robe of bright spray
He flung in my face,
Then down to the soles and the cods
With his sweet young grace.
Ah, what will the stripling learn,
From those rude mates that mountain burn,
What manners of th' extremely early gods?

IN MEMORIAM

HALF-MAST the flag by sweet St. Mary's shore,
Half-mast the schooner in Port Erin bay ;
Death has been with us in the night, of prey
Insatiate from a fold thrice robbed before.
And now he climbs to me upon the hoar
And ruinous rock, and shrouds the gladsome day
With sullen gloom, nor any word will say
That might to strength my sinking heart restore.
Speak, Death, O speak !   What high command restrains
The dark disclosure? is it thine own will
Thou workest, I adjure thee, shape of fear ?
Then from the awful face a shadow wanes,
And, clad in robes of light unspeakable,
God's loveliest angel sits beside me here.

SONG

Look at me, sun, ere thou set
    In the far sea ;
From the gold and the rose and the jet
    Look full at me !
Leave on my brow a trace
    Of tenderest light ;
Kiss me upon the face,
    Kiss for good-night.

DUNOON

LITTLE Maggie sitting in the pew,
Eyes of light and lips of dew !
What is that to you? what is that to you?
Little Maggie sitting in the pew.
Grinding like a saw-mill,
Worthy Doctor " Cawmill,"
What has he to do,
He so lank and prosy,
With Maggie plump and rosy—
Little Maggie sitting in the pew?
Is burd Maggie stupid?
No, by sweet Saint Cupid !
Rhythmic little sinner,
All that is within her
Chiming like a psalm

In the stellar calm.

Gracious warmth of blood

Making fancies bud

With a tender folly

Into belled corolle,

Radiating gleams

Of half-conscious dreams,

Floating her on blisses

Of potential kisses,

Filling all the presence

With a balmy pleasance,

With a kind confusion,

With a quick elusion

Of all ponderous matter

That would fain come at her

What is that to you,

Little Maggie, little Maggie, sitting in the pew?

Cubic, orthodox

Sink the ordered blocks,

Doctrinal adamant

Riven with the fiery rant,

And hammered with the hammer of John Knox ;

Cemented with the cant

Of glutinous emotion,

Compact with logic

Hard-gripped, presbyterous,

Something, mayhap, to us—

But Maggie, with a " mawgic "

Of which we have no notion,

Upborne upon the tide

Of her young life, has power to hide,

With unbroken sweetness

With a soul-completeness,

All the rock and rubble,

Knowing of no trouble,

Flecked only

With shadows of those lofty things and lonely

That from the seventh sphere

Pencil their diamond traces

Nowhere but on the mere

Of hearts that stir not from their places.

G

THE LAUGH

An empty laugh, I heard it on the road
    Shivering the twilight with its lance of mirth ;
And yet why empty? Knowing not its birth,
    This much I know, that it goes up to God :
And if to God, from God it surely starts,
    Who has within Himself the secret springs
    Of all the lovely, causeless, unclaimed things,
And loves them in His very heart of hearts.
A girl of fifteen summers, pure and free,
    Æolian, vocal to the lightest touch
Of fancy's winnowed breath — ah, happy such
    Whose life is music of the eternal sea.
Laugh on, laugh loud and long, O merry child,
    And be not careful to unearth a cause :
Thou art serenely placed above our laws,
    And we in thee with God are reconciled.

CLEVEDON VERSES

I

HALLAM'S CHURCH, CLEVEDON

A GRASSY field, the lambs, the nibbling sheep,
 A blackbird and a thorn, the April smile
 Of brooding peace, the gentle airs that wile
 The Channel of its moodiness; a steep
That brinks the flood, a little gate to keep
 The sacred ground—and then that old gray pile,
 A simple church wherein there is no guile
 Of ornament; and here the Hallams sleep.
Blest mourner, in whose soul the grief grew song,
 Not now, methinks, awakes the slumbering pain
 While Joy, with busy fingers, weaves the woof
Of Spring. But when the Winter nights are long,
 Thy spirit comes with sobbing of the rain,
 And spreads itself, and moans upon the roof.

II

DORA

She knelt upon her brother's grave,
 My little girl of six years old—
He used to be so good and brave,
 The sweetest lamb of all our fold ;
He used to shout, he used to sing,
Of all our tribe the little king
  And so unto the turf her ear she laid,
  To hark if still in that dark place he played.
   No sound ! no sound !
   Death's silence was profound ;
   And horror crept
   Into her aching heart, and Dora wept.
   If this is as it ought to be,
   My God, I leave it unto Thee.

III

SECUTURUS

Each night when I behold my bed
So fair outspread,
　　And all so soft and sweet—
　　Oh then above the folded sheet
His little coffin grows upon mine eye,
And I would gladly die.

IV

CUI BONO?

What comes
Of all my grief?　The Arabian grove
Is cut that costly gums[4]
May float into the nostrils of great Jove.
　　My heart resembles more a desert land—
Who cuts it cuts but rock, or digs the sapless sand.

V

STAR-STEERING

Oh will it ever come again
That I upon the boundless main
    Shall steer me by the light of stars?
    Now, locked with sandy bars,
 Life's narrowing channel bids me mark
Each serviceable spark
That Holm or Lundy flings upon the dark.
    Thus man is more to me—
    But oh the gladness of the outer sea!
    O Venus! Mars!
    When shall I steer by you again, O stars?

VI

PER OMNIA DEUS

What moves at Cardiff, how a man
At Newport ends the day as he began,
    At Weston what adventure may befall,
    What Bristol dreams, or if she dream at all,
Upon the pier, with step sedate,
I meditate—
    Poor souls ! whose God is Mammon.
Meanwhile, from Ocean's gate,
Keen for the foaming spate,
    The true God rushes in the salmon.

VII

Norton Wood (Dora's birthday)

In Norton wood the sun was bright,
In Norton wood the air was light,
    And meek anemonies,
    Kissed by the April breeze,
Were trembling left and right.
    Ah vigorous year !
    Ah primrose dear
    With smile so arch !
    Ah budding larch !
Ah hyacinth so blue,
We also must make free with you.
    Where are those cowslips hiding ?
    But we should not be chiding
The ground is covered every inch
What sayest, master finch ?
I see you on the swaying bough !
And very neat you are, I vow !
And Dora says it is " the happiest day ! '

Her birthday, hers!

And there's a jay,

  And from that clump of firs

Shoots a great pigeon, purple, blue, and gray.

  And, coming home,

  Well-laden, as we clomb

  Sweet Walton hill,

  A cuckoo shouted with a will—

"Cuckoo! cuckoo!" the first we've heard!

"Cuckoo! cuckoo!"   God bless the bird!

  Scarce time to take his breath,

And now "Cuckoo!" he saith—

Cuckoo! cuckoo! three cheers!

  And let the welkin ring!

  He has not folded wing

Since last he saw Algiers.

VIII

THE BRISTOL CHANNEL.

I

The sulky old gray brute!

But when the sunset strokes him,

Or twilight shadows coax him,

He gets so silver-milky,

He turns so soft and silky,

He'd make a water-spaniel for King Knut.

II

This sea was Lazarus, all day

At Dives' gate he lay,

And lapped the crumbs:

Night comes;

The beggar dies –

Forthwith the Channel, coast to coast,

Is Abraham's bosom; and the beggar lies

A lovely ghost.

IX

The Voices of Nature

This cluck of water in the tangles—

What said it to the Angles?

What to the Jutes

This wave sip-sopping round the salt sea-roots?

With what association did it hit on

The tympanum of a Damnonian Briton?

To tender Guinevere, to Britomart,

The stout of heart,

Along the guarded beach

Spoke it the same sad speech

It speaks to me—

This sopping of the sea?

Surely the plash

Of water upon stones,

Encountering in their ears the tones

Of dominant passions masterful,

Made but a bourdon for the chord

Of a great key, that rested lord

Of all the music, straining not the bones

Of Merlin's scull.

And in the ear of Vivian its frets

Were silver castanets,

That tinkled 'mong the vanities, and quickened

The free, full-blooded pulse,

Nor sickened

Her soul, nor stabbed her to the heart.

Strange! that to me this gurgling of the dulse

Allays no smart,

Consoles no nerve,

Rounds off no curve—

Alack!

Comes rather like a sigh,

A question that has no reply

Opens a deep misgiving

What is this life I'm living

Our fathers were not so—

Silence, thou moaning wrack!

And yet . . . I do not know .

And yet . . I would go back.

HOMINI ΔΗΜΙΟΤΡΓΟΣ

WHAT I can do I do, nor am I vexed,
Nor worn with aimless strife,
As you are, being perplexed
With suppositions, scribbling o'er the text
Of natural life.
And seeing that this is so,
And that I cannot know
The innumerous ills.
Therefore I strew the hills
And vallies with delight,
That, day or night,
In sad or merry plight,
You may catch sight
Of some sweet joy that thrills
Your heart.

And what if I impart
The same to frog or newt,
What if I steep the root
Of some old stump in bright vermilion,
And if the spider in his quaint pavilion
Catches a sunbeam where he thought a fly,
Ah, why
Should I not care for such?
I, who make all things, know it is not much.
And by analogy I must suppose
They have their woes
Like you:
Therefore I still must strew
Joys that may wait for centuries,
And light at last on Socrates,
Or on the frog, whose eyes
You may have noticed full of bright surprise.
Or have you not?   Ah then
You only think of men,
But I would have no single creature miss
One possible bliss.
And this
I certain: never be afraid!

I love what I have made.

I know this is not wit,

This is not to be clever,

Or anything whatever.

You see, I am a servant, that is it:

You've hit

The mark—a servant, for the other word—

Why you are Lord, if any one is Lord.

"NE SIT ANCILLÆ"

Poor little Teignmouth slavey,
    Squat, but rosy !
    Slatternly, but cosy,
A humble adjunct of the British navy,
A fifth rate dabbler in the British gravy —
    How was I mirrored? in what spiritual dress
    Appeared I to your struggling consciousness?

    Thump! bump!
    A dump
Of first a knife and then a fork,
    Then plump
A mustard pot, then slump, stump, frump,
    The plates
    Like slates

And lastly fearful wrestling with a cork.

   And so I thought—" Poor thing !

   She has not any wing

   To waft her from the grease,

   To give her soul release

   From this dull sphere

   Of baccy, beef, and beer."

   But, as it happed,

I spoke of Chagford, Chagford by the moor,

Sweet Chagford town.   Then pure

   And bright as Burton tapped

     By master hand,

   Then, red as is a peach,

   My little maid found speech—

   Gave me to understand

   She knew "them parts "—

     We stood elate,

As each revealed to each

     A mate—

     She stood, I sate,

And saw within her eyes

The folly of an infinite surprise.

H

LYNTON VERSES

I

May Margery of Lynton
  Is brighter than the day;
Her eye is like the sun in heaven
  Was ne'er so sweet a May.

May Margery has learnt a tune
  To which her soul is set
The voices of all happy things
  Are in its cadence met
The voices of all happy things
  In air, and earth, and sea,
Make music in the little breast
  Of sweet May Margery.

And has May Margery a heart?

   Nay, child, God give thee grace!

He made it for thee years ago,

   And keeps it in a place—

The heart of gold that shall be thine—

   But who shall have the key

That opens it—ah, who? ah, who?

   Ah, who, May Margery?

II

At Malmsmead, by the river side

   I met a little lady,

And, as she passed, she sang a song

   That was not Tait or Brady,

Or any song by art contrived

   Of minstrel or of poet,

For baron's hall, or chanter's desk;

   And yet I seemed to know it.

Good sooth! I think the song was mine—

   The all unthinking sadness—

She read it from my longing eyes,

   And gave it back in gladness.

And yet it was a challenge too,
    As plain as she could make it,
So petulant, so innocent,
    And yet I could not take it.
A breath, a gleam, and she is gone--
    Just half a minute only—
So die the breaths, so fade the gleams,
    And we are left so lonely.

III

Milk! milk! milk!
    Straight as the Parson's bands,
Streaming like silk
    Under and over her hands
        What is Mary scheming?
        What is Mary dreaming?

Swish! swish! swish!
    Pressing her sweet young brow
Smooth as a dish
    To the side of the sober cow
        Can she tell no tale then?
        Nought but milk and pail then?

Strip ! strip ! strip !

   Far away over the sea

Comes there a ship,

    The ship of all ships that be ?

      Ah little fairy !

      Ah Mary, Mary !

IV

LYNTON TO PORLOCK (Exmoor)

From Lynton when you drive to Porlock,

Just take old Tempus by the forelock—

In any case, don't hurry ; time and tide—

Of course—I know.   But, where the roads divide,

Upon the moor,

Be sure

To shun the *via dextra*,

And choose the marvellous ride

(One half-hour extra)

That zigzags to a gate

Nigh Porlock town—Oh it is great,

That strip of Channel sea,

Backed with the prime of English Arcady!

It is not that the heather rushes

In mad tumultous flushes

(*Trickling*'s the word I'd use);

But oh the greens and blues

And browns whereon the crimson dwells,

The buds, the bells;

The drop from arch to arch

Of pine and larch;

The scented glooms where soft sun-fainting culvers

Elude the eye,

And fox-gloves, like innumerous-celled revolvers

Shoot honey-tongued quintessence of July!

V

Sweet breeze that sett'st the summer buds a-swaying,

Dear lambs amid the primrose meadows playing,

　　Let me not think!

　　　O floods upon whose brink

The merry birds are maying,

Dream, softly dream!　O blessed mother, lead me

Unsevered from thy girdle—lead me ! feed me !

    I have no will but thine ;

       I need not but the juice

    Of elemental wine—

       Perish remoter use

Of strength reserved for conflict yet to come !

Let me be dumb,

    As long as I may feel thy hand -

    This, this is all—do ye not understand

How the great Mother mixes all our bloods ?

O breeze ! O swaying buds !

O lambs, O primroses, O floods !

VI

(SYMPHONY)

Adagio.

We saw her die, and she is dead—

    Our little sister—

    A March wind came and kissed her,

And sighed and fled—

    Beyond the hill,

    Far in the East we hear him sighing still.

But she is dead

Our little sister's dead!

　　Ah, chill! chill! chill!

Ah, see the drooping head.

Our sister's dead —

We know that she is dead.

Andante con moto.

Talitha cumi!　O Thou Christ,

Hast kept the tryst?

Laugh not, O maidens! this is He

Of Galilee,

Of Nazareth.

The Christ that conquers Death

Dost catch a breath,

O Christ?　O Life!

Talitha cumi!　See

The tumult as of some sweet strife

Strained tremulous up up

"Give her to drink!" He saith

Yea, Lord, behold, a cup!

Scherzo.

O gentle airs of Spring,

Come to the hills and the valleys,

From the South, from the West,

As seems you best,

    Rocked in your golden galleys.

Bring the bread, bring the wine,

Bring the smell that's fine,

Bring the scarf, and the bright green wimple !

See, she dips ! see, she sips ! put your oozy lips

    To the curve of each nascent dimple—

To her head, to her feet

So warm and sweet

    Bring the rain and the sunshine after ;

To the ordered limbs

Where the new life swims,

To the kneaded mesh

Of the soft pink flesh

Bring baths of dew,

Bring skies of blue—

    Bring love, and light, and laughter !

Trio.

Goldfinch underneath the bough

    Clinging, swinging,

You are happy now.

Blackbird, as you flit along,

Staying, swaying,

Sing her but one song!

Dove, when twilight wakes unrest,

Yearning, burning,

Lean to her your breast!

Finale.

O God of Heaven!

These are Thy gifts, to all Thy creatures given—

Love, laughter, light

'Stablish the ancient right,

O God; and bend above them all Thy brooding arch—

Dove, blackbird, goldfinch, larch!

THE EMPTY CUP

Fly away, bark,
  Over the sea;
Take thou my grief,
  Take it with thee!
Bear it afar
  Unto the shore
Where the old griefs are
  For evermore.
Oh it was hard!
  Take it away—
Pressed on my heart
  By night and by day.
I will not have it;
  Let it go, let it go!
Shall I have nothing
  But wailing and woe?

Let it be, let it be !
   Oh bring it again :
Bring my sorrow to me,
   Bring weeping and pain.
Bring my sorrow to me
   After all, it is mine :
O God of my heart,
   I will not repine.
For I feel such a lack,
   And I am such a stone
Bring it back, bring it back
   It is better to groan
With my old old load
   Than to search within,
And find nothing there
   But folly and sin.
Oh I cannot bear
   This empty cup :
If it must be with gall,
   Fill it up ! fill it up '
Fill my soul, fill my soul !
   And I will bless
The hand that filleth
   Mine emptiness.

PAIN

THE man that hath great griefs I pity not ;
   ' Tis something to be great
   In any wise, and hint the larger state,
Though but in shadow of a shade, God wot !

Moreover, while we wait the possible,
   This man has touched the fact,
   And probed till he has felt the core, where, packed
In pulpy folds, resides the ironic ill.

And while we others sip the obvious sweet—
   Lip-licking after-taste
   Of glutinous rind, lo ! this man hath made haste,
And pressed the sting that holds the central seat.

For thus it is God stings us into life,
   Provoking actual souls
   From bodily systems, giving us the poles
That are His own, not merely balanced strife.

Nay, the great passions are His veriest thought,
   Which whoso can absorb,
   Nor, querulous halting, violate their orb,
In him the mind of God is fullest wrought.

Thrice happy such an one! far other he
   Who dallies on the edge
   Of the great vortex, clinging to a sedge
Of patent good, a timorous Manichee,

Who takes the impact of a long breathed force,
   And fritters it away
   In eddies of disgust, that else might stay
His nerveless heart, and fix it to the course.

For there is threefold oneness with the one:
   And he is one, who keeps
   The homely laws of life; who, if he sleeps,
Or wakes, in his true flesh God's will is done

And he is one, who takes the deathless forms,

    Who schools himself to think

    With the All-thinking, holding fast the link

God-riveted that bridges casual storms.

But tenfold one is he, who feels all pains

    Not partial, knowing them

    As ripples parted from the gold-beaked stem

Wherewith God's galley onward ever strains.

To him the sorrows are the tension-thrills

    Of that serene endeavour

    Which yields to God for ever and for ever

The joy that is more ancient than the hills.

THE PITCHER

OFTEN at a wayside fountain
  You may see a pitcher stand,
Stooped beneath the mossy channel,
  Purple slate on either hand.

And the streamlet, never heeding
  If the pitcher's brimming o'er,
With an innocent penitence
  Lavishes its silver store.

And the crystal-beaded bubbles
  Burst upon its lazy lip ;
But the well contented pitcher
  Does not even care to sip ;

Does not even know that o'er him
  There is flowing from the hill
What would fill a thousand pitchers,
  And a thousand pitchers still.

Wasted on his gurgling fulness
  All its fretting soft and faint,
Wasted all its pretty urging,
  All the music of its plaint !

But the streamlet, ever patient,
  Ceaseless laves his churlish sides ;
For the streamlet has the patience
  That in Nature's heart abides.

Even so at God's sweet fountain
  Some one left me long ago ;
Left my shallow soul expectant
  Of the everlasting flow.

And it came, and poured upon me,
  Rose and mantled to the brim ;
And I knew that God was filling
  One more soul to carry Him.

I

So He filled me—then I lost Him,
 Lost Him in His own excess;
For He could not but transcend me
 In my very nothingness.

Wretched soul! that could'st not hold Him,
 Soul incapable and base!
Hardly 'ware that He doth bathe thee
 Steeped in largess of His grace!

Puny soul! that could'st not take Him,
 Torpid soul—that feel'st no need!
Perish from before the Godhead,
 Let a larger soul succeed!

" Not so!" saith the God of goodness;
 " I have many souls to fill;
From this soul a while desisting,
 I will tarry in the hill.

" Then, when it is dry and dusty,
 I will seek the thirsty plain;
I will wet the mossy channel,
 And the purple slate again."

SONG

"WEARY wind of the West
    Over the billowy sea—
Come to my heart, and rest!
    Ah, rest with me!
Come from the distance dim
    Bearing the sun's last sigh;
I hear thee sobbing for him
    Through all the sky."

So the wind came,
    Purpling the middle sea,
Crisping the ripples of flame—
    Came unto me;
Came with a rush to the shore,
    Came with a bound to the hill,
Fell, and died at my feet—
    Then all was still.

VERIS ET FAVONI

Sing, Zephyr, sing
Shed from your dusky wing
  The violets.
  Make music with your golden frets—
Sing, Zephyr, sing !

Sigh, Zephyr, sigh !
Give passion to the sky '
  The tawny south
  Has no such odorous mouth -
Sigh, Zephyr, sigh !

Sue, Zephyr, sue !
Bring earth the sunny blue,
  The pearly mist
  With new born love fire kissed
Sue, Zephyr, sue !

Sip, Zephyr, sip!

The primrose lends her lip,

    The crocus thrills ;

    Love hides among the daffodils—

Sip, Zephyr, sip!

Seek, Zephyr, seek!

The vermeil of my lady's cheek!

    So seeking, sipping, suing, sighing, singing,

    While old Time his flight is winging,

Tell her to be

Most kind to me.

IN GREMIO

"Come unto God!" I heard a preacher call:
    Immediate God to me,
Who in His bosom lay—"Mind not at all
    Such accidents as he—
Mechanical alarum, sightless seer,
Who bids thee come, and knows not thou art here."

IBANT OBSCURÆ

To-night I saw three maidens on the beach,
    Dark-robed descending to the sea,
So slow, so silent of all speech,
    And visible to me
Only by that strange drift-light, dim, forlorn,
Of the sun's wreck, and clashing surges born.

Each after other went,
    And they were gathered to his breast—
It seemed to me a sacrament
    Of some stern creed unblest ;
As when to rocks, that cheerless girt the bay,
They bound thy holy limbs, Andromeda.

ST. BEE'S HEAD

I HAVE seen cliffs that met the ocean foe
    As a black bison, with his crouching front
    And neck back-coiled, awaits the yelping hunt
That reck not of his horns protruding low.

And others I have seen with calm disdain
    O'erlook the immediate strife, and gaze afar ;
    Eternity was in that gaze ; the jar
Of temporal broil assailed not its domain.

Some cliffs are full of pity ; in the sweep
    Of their bluff brows a kindly tolerance waits,
    And smiles upon the petulant sea, that rates,
And fumes, and scolds against the patient steep.

And some are joyous with a hearty joy,

     And in mock-earnest wage the busy fight :

     So may you see a giant with delight

Parrying the buffets of a saucy boy.

Remonstrant others stand—a wild surprise

     Glares from their crests against the insolent throng ;

     Half frightened, half indignant at the wrong,

They look appealing to those heedless skies.

And other some are of a sleepy mood,

     Who care not if the tempest does its worst ;

     What is't to them if bounding billows burst,

Or winds assail them with their jeerings rude ?

But like not unto any one of these

     Is that tall crag that northward guards the bay,

     And stands a watchful sentry night and day

Above the pleasant downs of old St. Bee's.

                   •

Straight-levelled as the bayonet's dread array

     His shelves abide the charge ; come one, come all !

     The blustering surges at his feet shall fall

And writhe and sob their puny lives away.

AN OXFORD IDYLL

An little mill, you're rumbling still,
    Ah sunset flecked with gold !
Ah deepening tinge, ah purple fringe
    Of lilac as of old !
Ah hawthorn hedge, ah light-won pledge
    Of kisses warm and plenty,
When she was true, and twenty-two,
    And I was two-and-twenty.
I don't know how she broke her vow—
    She said that I was "horty";
And there's the mill "a-goin' still,
    And I am five and forty.
And sooth to tell, 'twas just as well,
    Her aitches were uncertain ;
Her ways though nice, not point device ;
    Her father liked his " Burton."

But there's a place you cannot trace,
　　So spare the fond endeavour--
A cloudless sky, where Kate and I
　　Are twenty-two for ever.

MAGDALEN WALK.

THE SCHOONER

Just mark that schooner westward far at sea—
      'Tis but an hour ago
When she was lying hoggish at the quay,
      And men ran to and fro,
And tugged, and stamped, and shoved, and pushed, and
          swore,
And ever and anon, with crapulous glee,
Grinned homage to viragoes on the shore.

So to the jetty gradual she was hauled :
      Then one the tiller took,
And chewed, and spat upon his hand, and bawled ;
      And one the canvas shook
Forth like a mouldy bat ; and one, with nods
And smiles, lay on the bowsprit-end, and called
And cursed the Harbour-master by his gods.

And, rotten from the gunwhale to the keel,

    Rat-riddled, bilge bestank,

Slime-slobbered, horrible, I saw her reel,

    And drag her oozy flank,

And sprawl among the deft young waves, that laughed,

And leapt, and turned in many a sportive wheel,

As she thumped onward with her lumbering draught.

And now, behold! a shadow of repose

    Upon the line of gray

She sleeps, that transverse cuts the evening rose

    She sleeps, and dreams away,

Soft-blended in a unity of rest

All jars, and strifes obscene, and turbulent throes

'Neath the broad benediction of the West—

Sleeps; and methinks she changes as she sleeps,

    And dies, and is a spirit pure;

Lo! on her deck an angel pilot keeps

    His lonely watch secure;

And at the entrance of Heaven's dockyard waits

Till from Night's leash the fine-breath'd morning leaps,

And that strong hand within unbars the gates.

WHITEHAVEN HARBOUR

On' can't she?   Listen! there's a volley!
   Stand to your guns, my Ipswich boy!
   Chain-shot ahoy!
" Ah, ain't she jolly
   (Young Ipswich telegraphing
   To us upon the quay)!
   Some credit chaffing
   With her!"   Decidedly—
" The gen'lemen are looking."   Yes, we are,
My noble Ipswich tar—
   " Ain't her eyes brown?
   (Says telegraph)
   Ah, can't she laugh?
And ain't she all so nice and pert? '
Yes, yes! stand up and flirt!

Flirt for the honour of your native town !

Flirt ! flirt ! my man of Ipswich.   Not so bad !

A good sufficient lad !

See how the strong young hearts

Dance to the tongue-tips ; lightning darts

From eye to eye :

The maiden is not shy !

See the two Manxmen on the schooner there,

Who stare

With all their souls in silent admiration

Of such a very excellent flirtation !

Quite out of it—

Those Manxmen—wait a bit—

Poor fellows !   Shall we hail them ?   No ?

Ah well, let's go.

SCARLETT ROCKS

I thought of life, the outer and the inner,
 As I was walking by the sea,
How vague, unshapen this, and that, though thinner,
 Yet hard and clear in its rigidity.
Then took I up the fragment of a shell,
 And saw its accurate loveliness,
And searched its filmy lines, its pearly cell,
 And all that keen contention to express
A finite thought.   And then I recognised
 God's working in the shell from root to rim,
And said   " He works till He has realised—
 Oh Heaven ! if I could only work like Him ! "

LIME STREET

You might have been as lovely as the dawn,
Had household sweetness nurtured you, and arts
Domestic, and the strength which love imparts
To lowliness, and chastened ardour drawn
From vital sap that burgeons in the brawn
Around the dreadful arms of Hercules,
And shapes the curvature of Dian's knees,
And has its course in lilies of the lawn.
Even now your flesh is soft and full, defaced
Although it be, and bruised.   Unblenched your eyes
Meet mine, as misinterpreting their call,
Then sink, reluctant forced to recognise
That there are men whose look is not unchaste—
O God! the pain! the horror of it all!

K

HOTWELLS

Is it her face that looks from forth the glare
    Of those dull stony eyes?
    Her face! that used to light with meek surprise,
If I but said that she was fair!

Can it have come to this since at the gate
    Her lips between the bars
Fluttered irresolute to mine, for it was late
    Beneath the misty stars!

It was our last farewell, our last farewell
    O heaven above!
And now she is a fearful thing of Hell
    My dove! my dove!
A hollow thing carved rigid on the shell
    Of her that was my love'

Yet, if the soul remain,

    There crouched and dumb behind the obdurate mask,

    This would I ask—

Kill her, O God! that so, the flesh being slain,

Her soul my soul may be again.

BRADDAN VICARAGE

I WONDER if in that far isle,
     Some child is growing now, like me
When I was child, care pricked, yet healed the while
     With balm of rock and sea.

I wonder if the purple ring
     That rises on a belt of blue
Provokes the little bashful thing
     To guess what may ensue
When he has pierced the screen, and holds the further clue.

I wonder if beyond the verge
     He dim conjectures England's coast,
The land of Edwards and of Henries, scourge
     Of insolent foemen, at the most
Faint caught where Cumbria looms a geographic ghost.

I wonder if to him the sycamore

    Is full of green and tender light,

If the gnarled ash stands stunted at the door,

    By salt sea-blast defrauded of its right,

If budding larches feed the hunger of his sight.

I wonder if to him the dewy globes

    Like mercury nestle in the caper leaf,

If, when the white narcissus dons its robes,

    It soothes his childish grief,

If silver plates the birch, gold rustles in the sheaf.

I wonder if to him the heath-clad mountain

    With crimson pigment fills the sensuous cells,

If like full bubbles from an emerald fountain

    Gorse bloom luxuriant wells,

If God with trenchant forms the insolent lushness quells.

I wonder if the hills are long and lonely

    That North from South divide ;

I wonder if he thinks that it is only

    The hither slope where men abide,

Unto all mortal homes refused the other side.

I wonder if some day he, chance-conducted,

    Attains the vantage of the utmost height,

And, by his own discovery instructed,

    Sees grassy plain, and cottage white,

Each human sign and pledge that feeds him with delight.

At eventide, when lads with lasses dally,

    And milking Pei sits singing at the pail,

I wonder if he hears along the valley

    The wind's sad sough, half credulous of the tale

How from Slieu-whallan moans the murdered witches' wail.

I wonder if to him "the boat" descending

    From the proud East his spirit fills

With a strange joy, adventurous ardour lending

    To the mute soul that thrills

As booms the herald gun, and westward wakes the hills.

I wonder if he loves that Captain bold

    Who has the horny hand,

Who swears the mighty oath, who well can hold,

    Half drunk, serene command,

And guide his straining bark to refuge of the land.

I wonder if he thinks the world has aught
    Of strong, or nobly wise,
Like him by whom the invisible land is caught
    With instinct true, nor storms, nor midnight skies
Avert the settled aim, or daunt the keen emprise.

I wonder if he deems the English men
    A higher type beyond his reach,
Imperial blood by Heaven ordained with pen
    And sword the populous world to teach ;
If awed he hears the tones as of an alien speech :

Or, older grown, suspects a braggart race,
    Ignores phlegmatic claim
Of privileged assumption, holding base
    Their technic skill and aim,
And all the prosperous fraud that binds their social frame.

Young rebel ! how he pants, who knows not what
    He hates, yet hates, all one to him
If Guleph, or Buonaparte, or sans-culotte,
    If Strafford or if Pym
Usurp the clumsy helm, if England sink or swim.

Ah crude, undisciplined, when thou shalt know
What good is in this England, still of joys
The chiefest count it thou wast nurtured so
That thou may'st keep the larger equipoise,
And stand outside these nations and their noise.

TO K. H.

O far withdrawn into the lonely West,
　To whom those Irish hills are as a grave
　　　Cairn-crowned, the dead sun's monument,
And this fair English land but vaguely guessed—
　Thee, lady, by the melancholy wave
　　　I greet where salt winds whistle through the bent,
And harsh sea-holly buds beneath thy foot are pressed.

What is thy thought? 'tis not the obvious scene
　That holds thee with its grand simplicity
　　　Of natural forms; thou musest rather
What larger life may be, what richer sheen
　Of social gloss in lands beyond the sea,
　　　What nobler cult than where around thy father
The silent fishers pray in chapel small and mean.

Yes, thou art absent far – thy soul has slipt

   The visual bond, and thou art lowly kneeling

      Upon a pavement with the sacred kisses

Of emerald and ruby gleamings lipped :

   And down the tunnelled nave the organ pealing

      Blows music-storm, and with far-floating blisses

Gives tremor to the bells, and shakes the dead men's crypt.

This is thy thought ; for this thou heav'st the sigh :

   Yet, lady, look around thee ! hast thou not

      The life of real men, the home,

The tribe, and for a temple that old sky ?

   Whereto the sea intones the polyglot

      Of water-pipes antiphonal, and the dome

Round-arched goes up to God in lapis lazuli ?

CLIFTON

I'm here at Clifton, grinding at the mill
    My feet for thrice nine barren years have trod,
But there are rocks and waves at Scarlett still,
    And gorse runs riot in Glen Chass—thank God!

Alert, I seek exactitude of rule,
    I step, and square my shoulders with the squad,
But there are blaeberries on old Barrule,
    And Langness has its heather still—thank God!

There is no silence here : the truculent quack
    Insists with acrid shriek my ears to prod,
And, if I stop them, fumes ; but there's no lack
    Of silence still on Carraghyn—thank God!

Pragmatic fibs surround my soul, and bate it
  With measured phrase that asks the assenting nod ;
I rise, and say the bitter thing, and hate it,
  But Wordsworth's castle's still at Peel — thank God !

Oh, broken life ! oh wretched bits of being,
  Unrhythmic patched, the even and the odd !
But Bradda still has lichens worth the seeing,
  And thunder in her caves—thank God ! thank God !

THE LILY-POOL

WHAT sees our mailie in the lily-pool,

    What sees she with that large surprise?

What sees our mailie in the lily-pool

    With all the violet of her big eyes—

      Our mailie in the lily-pool?

She sees herself within the lily-pool,

    Herself in flakes of brown and white,

Herself beneath the slab that is the lily-pool,

    The green and liquid slab of light

    With cups of silver dight,

    Stem-rooted in the depths of amber night

That hold the hollows of the lily-pool—

      Our own dear lily-pool.

And does she gaze into the lily-pool

    As one that is enchanted?

Or does she try the cause to find

    How the reflection's slanted

That sleeps within the lily-pool?

    Or does she take it all for granted,

With the sweet natural logic of her kind?

    The lazy logic of the lily-pool,

    Our own bright, innocent, stupid lily-pool!

She knows that it is nice—our lily-pool;

    She likes the water-rings around her knees,

    She likes the shadow of the trees

That droop above the lily-pool;

    She likes to scatter with a silly sneeze

The long-legged flies that skim the lily-pool--

The peaceful-sleeping baby lily-pool.

So may I look upon the lily-pool,

    Nor ever in the slightest care

    Why I am there;

Why upon land and sea

Is ever stamped the inevitable me ·

But rather say with that most gentle fool—

" How pleasant is this lily-pool !

How nice and cool !

Be off, you long-legged flies ! oh what a spree !

To drive the flies from off the lily-pool !

From off this most sufficient, absolute lily-pool ! "

"NOT WILLING TO STAY"

I saw a fisher bold yestreen
    At his cottage by the bay,
And I asked how he and his had been
    While I was far away.
But when I asked him of the child
    With whom I used to play,
The sunniest thing that ever smiled
    Upon a summer's day
Then said that fisher bold to me
    And turned his face away
"She was not willing to stay with us
    She was not willing to stay."

" But, Evan, she was brave and strong,
    And blithesome as the May ;
And who would do her any wrong,
    Our darling of the bay ? "

His head was low, his breath was short,
    He seemed as he would pray,
Nor answer made in any sort
    That might his grief betray;
Save once again that fisher bold
    Turned and to me did say-
"She was not willing to stay with us,
    She was not willing to stay."

Then I looked upon his pretty cot
    So neat in its array,
And I looked upon his garden-plot
    With its flowers so trim and gay :
And I said—" He hath no need of me
    To help him up the brae ;
God worketh in his heart, and He
    Will soon let in the day."
So I left him there, and sought yon rock
    Where leaps the salt sea-spray ;
For ah ! how many have lost their loves
    That were "not willing to stay " with them,
That were not willing to stay !

L

ECCLESIASTES

WE came from church, she from the Down was coming,
    She with a branch of may,
We laden with persistence of the humming
    Wherein men think they pray :
She winning to her faded face a beauty
From the kissed buds, we having heard " the duty
    Performed " with needful prayer-book thumbing,
    We *proper*, she so gay.

Yet, as we met, her little joy was dashed
    By our spruce decency :
She hung her head as who must be abashed
    In her poor liberty,
Forgetting how in that damp city cellar
The sick child pines whom none but God did tell her
    To bring bright flowers Himself has splashed
    With dew for such as she.

Or was it but the natural rebound

    To what thou truly art,

O worn with life ! whose soul-depths He would sound,

    And prick upon His chart?

Is this thy "service"?   Stay! for very grace!

One moment stay, and lift the faded face !

    O woman ! woman ! thou hast found

    The way into my heart.

MATER DOLOROSA

Aw, Billy, good sowl! don't cuss! don't cuss!

Ye see, these angels is grand to nuss;

And it's lek they're feedin them on some nice air,

Or dew or the lek, that's handy there,

O Billy, look at my poor poor bress!

O Billy, see the full it is!

But . . . O my God! . . . but navar mind!

There's no doubt them sperrits is very kind—

And of coorse they're that beautiful it's lekly

The childher is takin to them directly

Eh, Billy, eh? . . . And . . . oh my head!

Billy, Billy, come to bed! . . .

And the little things that navar knew sin

And everything as nate as a pin:

And the lovely bells goin ding a lingin

And of coorse we've allis heard of their singin.

But won't he want me when he'll be wakin?

Will they take him up when he's wantin takin?

I hope he'll not be left in the dark—

He was allis used to make a wark

If a body 'd lave him the smallest minute—

Dear me! the little linnet—

But I forgot—it's allis light

In yandhar place . . . all right! all right!

I forgot, ye see, . . . I'm not very well . . .

Light, was I sayin? but who can tell?

Bad for the eyes though . . . but a little curtain

On a string, ye know—aw certain! certain!

Let me feel your face, Billy! Just us two!

Aw, Billy, the sorry I am for you!

Aw 'deed it is, Billy,—very disthressin

To lave your childher to another pessin—

But . . . all the little rooms that's theer- -

And Jesus walkin up the steer,

And tappin lek—I see! I see!—

O Jesus Christ, have pity on me!

But He'll come, He'll come! He'll give a look

Just to see the care that's took—

Oh there's no doubt He's very gud—

Oh I think He wud, I think He wud !

But still . . . but still . . . but I don't know

O Billy, I think I'd like to go-

What's that, Billy? did ye hear a cry?

O Illiam, the sweet it 'd be to die !

INDWELLING

I‌f thou couldst empty all thyself of self,

 Like to a shell dishabited,

Then might He find thee on the Ocean shelf,

 And say—"This is not dead,"--

And fill thee with Himself instead.

But thou art all replete with very *thou*,

 And hast such shrewd activity,

That, when He comes, He says—"This is enow

 Unto itself—'Twere better let it be :

It is so small and full, there is no room for Me."

EXILE

In sorrow and in nakedness of soul
    I look into the street,
    If haply there mine eye may meet
As up and down it ranges,
The servants of my father bearing changes
    Of raiment sweet
Seven changes sweet with violet and moly,
Seven changes pure and holy.

But nowhere 'mid the thick entangled throng
    Mark I their proud sad paces,
    Nowhere the light upon their faces
Serene with that great beauty
Wherein the singly meditated duty
    Its empire traces : -

Only the fretful merchants stand and cry—
"Come buy! come buy! come buy!"

And the big bales are drunk with all the purple
    That wells in vats of Tyre,
    And unrolled damasks stream with golden fire,
And broideries of Ind,
And, piled on Polar furs, are braveries winned
    From far Gadire.
And I am waiting, abject, cold, and numb,
Yet sure that they will come.

O naked soul, be patient in this stead!
    Thrice blest are they that wait.
    O Father of my soul, the gate
Will open soon, and they
Who minister to Thee and Thine alway
    Will enter straight,
And speak to me that I shall understand
The speech of Thy great land.

And I will rise, and wash, and they will dress me
    As Thou would'st have me dressed;

And I shall stand confest
Thy son ; and men shall falter
" Behold the ephod of the unseen altar !
            O God-possessed !
Thy raiment is not from the looms of earth,
But has a Heavenly birth."

SALVE!

To live within a cave—it is most good ;

    But, if God make a day,

    And some one come, and say—

" Lo ! I have gathered faggots in the wood ! "

    E'en let him stay,

And light a fire, and fan a temporal mood !

So sit till morning ! when the light is grown

    That he the path can read,

    Then bid the man God-speed !

His morning is not thine : yet must thou own

They have a cheerful warmth—those ashes on the stone.

IN MEMORIAM

PAUL BRIDSON

TAKE him, O Braddan, for he loved thee well—
    Take him, kind mother of my own dear dead!
        And let him lay his head
            On thy soft breast,
                And rest
                    Rest !

He loved thee well ; and thee, my father, thee
    Also he loved.   Oh, meet him ! reassure
        That heart thou prov'dst so pure
            Whisper release !
                And peace
                    Peace '

O countrymen, believe me ! here is laid

  A Manxman's heart the simplest and the truest :

    O Spring, when thou renewest

      Thy sunny hours,

        Bring flowers—

          Flowers !

  And bring them of thy sweetest

  And bring them of thy meetest

  And, till God's trumpet wake him,

  Take him, O Braddan, take him !

CLIMBING

When I would get me to the upper fields,
　　　I look if anywhere
A man be found who craves what joyaunce yields
　　　The keen thin air,
Who loves the rapture of the height,
And fain would snatch with me a perilous delight.

I wait, and linger on the village street,
　　　And long for one to come,
And say "The morning's bright, it is not meet
　　　That thou the hum
Of vulgar life shouldst leave, and seek the view
Alone from those great peaks ; I surely will go too.

But not to me comes ever any man ;

    Or, if he come, dull sleep

Still thickens in his eyes, so that to scan

    The beckoning steep

He has no power ; and of its scornful cone

Unconscious sits him down, and I go on alone.

Yet children are before me on the slope,

    Their dew-bedabbled prints

Press the black fern-roots naked ; sunny hope

    Darts red, and glints

Upon their hair ; but, devious, they remain

Among the bilberry beds, and I go on again.

And so there is no help for it, no mate

    To share the arduous way :

Natheless I must ascend ere it grow late,

    And, dim and gray,

The final cloud obstruct my soul's endeavour,

And I see nothing more for ever and for ever.

IN MEMORIAM A. F.

Ob. Oct. 12, 1879.

Aug. 1875.

BRIGHT skies, bright sea-

    All happy things

    That, borne on wings,

Cleave the long distance, glad and free-

    A boat swift swirls

    Of foam-wake—boys and girls

And innocence and laughter She

Was there, and was so happy ; and I said—-

"God bless the children!"

Oct. 1879.

        Dead!

Dead, say you ? "Yes, the last sweet rose

Is gathered Close, oh close,

Oh gently, gently, very gently close

Her little book of life, and seal it up

To God, who gave, who took- -oh bitter cup !

Oh bell !

O folding grave—O mother, it is well—

Yes, it is well.   He holds the key

That opens all the mysteries ; and He

Has blessed our children—it is well.

M

RISUS DEI

METHINKS in Him there dwells alway
    A sea of laughter very deep,
    Where the leviathans leap,
And little children play,
Their white feet twinkling on its crisped
    edge,
But in the outer bay
The strong man drives the wedge
    Of polished limbs,
    And swims.
Yet there is one will say
" It is but shallow, neither is it broad " -
And so he frowns ; but is he nearer
    God ?

One saith that God is in the note of bird,

    And piping wind, and brook,

And all the joyful things that speak no word :

    Then if from sunny nook

Or shade a fair child's laugh

    Is heard,

Is not God half?

And if a strong man gird

His loins for laughter, stirred

By trick of ape or calf—

    Is he no better than a cawing rook ?

Nay 'tis a Godlike function ; laugh thy fill !

    Mirth comes to thee unsought ;

Mirth sweeps before it like a flood the mill

    Of languaged logic ; thought

Hath not its source so high ;

    The will

Must let it by :

    For though the heavens are still,

    God sits upon His hill,

And sees the shadows fly ;

    And if He laughs at fools, why should He not ?

"Yet hath a fool a laugh"—Yea, of a sort ;
        God careth for the fools ;
        The chemic tools
Of laughter He hath given them, and some toys
        Of sense, as 'twere a small retort
Wherein they may collect the joys
Of natural giggling, as becomes their state :
        The fool is not inhuman, making sport
For such as would not gladly be without
That old familiar noise.
Since, though he laugh not, he can cachinnate —
This also is of God, we may not doubt.

"Is there an empty laugh ?"   Best called a shell
        From which a laugh has flown,
A mask, a well
        That hath no water of its own,
        Part echo of a groan,
        Which, if it hide a cheat,
        Is a base counterfeit ;
        But if one borrow
        A cloak to wrap a sorrow
        That it may pass unknown,

Then can it not be empty.   God doth dwell
    Behind the feigned gladness,
    Inhabiting a sacred core of sadness.

" Yet is there not an evil laugh ? "   Content—
    What follows ?
    When Satan fills the hollows
    Of his bolt-riven heart
    With spasms of unrest,
And calls it laughter ; if it give relief
To his great grief,
    Grudge not the dreadful jest.
But if the laugh be aimed
At any good thing that it be ashamed,
    And blush thereafter,
    Then it is evil, and it is not laughter.

There are who laugh, but know not why,
    Whether the force
    Of simple health and vigour seeks a course
Extravagant, as when a wave runs high,
And tips with crest of foam the incontinent curve,
Or if it be reserve

Of power collected for a goal, which had,
Behold ! the man is fresh.　So when strung nerve,
　　Stout heart, pent breath, have brought you to the
　　　　source
Of a great river, on the topmost stie
　　Of cliff, then have you had
All heaven to laugh with you ; yet somewhere nigh
　　A shepherd lad
　　Has wondering looked, and deemed that you were
　　　　mad.

THE PRAYERS

I was in Heaven one day when all the prayers
Came in, and angels bore them up the stairs
    Unto a place where he
    Who was ordained such ministry
Should sort them so that in that palace bright
The presence-chamber might be duly dight ;
For they were like to flowers of various bloom ;
And a divinest fragrance filled the room.

Then did I see how the great sorter chose
One flower that seemed to me a hedgeling rose,
    And from the tangled press
    Of that irregular loveliness

Set it apart—and—"This," I heard him say,

" Is for the Master": so upon his way

He would have passed; then I to him—

"Whence is this rose?   O thou of cherubim

The chiefest?"—"Know'st thou not?" he said and smiled,

"This is the first prayer of a little child."

IN A FAIR GARDEN

In a fair garden

    I saw a mother playing with her child,

    And with that chance beguiled

    I could not choose but look

How she did seem to harden

    His little soul to brook

    Her absence—reconciled

    With after boon of kisses,

    And sweet irrational blisses.

For she would hide

    With loveliest grace

    Of seeming craft

Till he was ware of none beside

    Himself upon the place :—

    And then he laughed ;

And then he stood a space

Disturbed, his face

Prepared for tears ;

And half-acknowledged fears

Met would-be courage, balancing

His heart upon the spring

Of flight   till, waxing stout,

He gulped the doubt.

So up the pleached alley

Full swift he ran :

Whence she,

Not long delayed,

Rushed forth with joyous sally

Upon her little man.

Then was it good to see

How each to other made

A pretty rapture of discovery.

Blest child ! blest mother ! blest the truth ye taught—

God seeketh us, and yet He would be sought.

CANTICLE

WHEN all the sky is pure
  My soul takes flight,
Serene and sure,
    Upward—till at the height
      She weighs her wings,
        And sings.

But when the heaven is black,
    And west-winds sigh,
Beat back, beat back,
      She has no strength to try
        The drifting rain
          Again.

So cheaply baffled! see!

The field is bare

Behold a tree--

Is't not enough?   Sit there,

Thou foolish thing!

And sing!

EUROCLYDON

SCARCE loosed from Crete—
    Then, borne on wings of flame
And sleet
    The Euroclydon came.

Strained yard, bent mast,
    With fury of his mouth
The blast
    Compels us to the South.

Canst see, for spume
    And mist, and writhen air,
A loom
    Of Clauda anywhere ?

Balked hopes, fooled wit !

    Ah soul, to gain this loss,

Didst quit

    The shelter of His cross?

Dear Lord, if thou

    Would'st walk upon the sea,

My prow

    Unblenched should turn to Thee.

Wind roars, wave yelps—

    To Thy blest side I'd slip,

Use helps,

    And undergird the ship.

DISGUISES

HIGH stretched upon the swinging yard,

    I gather in the sheet ;

But it is hard

    And stiff, and one cries haste :—

Then He that is most dear in my regard

    Of all the crew gives aidance meet :

    But from His hands, and from His feet,

A glory spreads wherewith the night is starred :

    Moreover of a cup most bitter-sweet

With fragrance as of nard,

And myrrh, and cassia spiced,

    He proffers me to taste.

Then I to Him—" Art Thou the Christ ? "

    He saith—" Thou say'st."

Like to an ox
    That staggers 'neath the mortal blow,
She grinds upon the rocks :
    Then straight and low
Leaps forth the levelled line, and in our quarter locks.
The cradle's rigged ; with swerving of the blast
      We go,
Our Captain last—
      Demands
       "Who fired that shot?"   Each silent stands—
Ah sweet perplexity !
This too was He.

    I have an arbour wherein came a toad
      Most hideous to see
Immediate, seizing staff or goad,
      I smote it cruelly.
Then all the place with subtle radiance glowed
      I looked, and it was He !

MY GARDEN

A GARDEN is a lovesome thing, God wot !

Rose plot,

   Fringed pool,

Ferned grot—

   The veriest school

   Of peace ; and yet the fool

Contends that God is not—

Not God ! in gardens ! when the eve is cool ?

   Nay, but I have a sign ;

   'Tis very sure God walks in mine.

N

RECONCILIATION

THERE is a place where He hath split the hills ;
No water fills
        The gap :—
            A bow-shot wide
            Side stands to side.
        Indenture perfectly opposed,
        The outlet closed
        By seeming overlap
So severed are our hearts, so rent our wills ;
And yet the old correlatives remain
Ah ! brother, may we not be joined again ?

LAND, HO!

I know 'tis but a loom of land,
Yet is it land, and so I will rejoice,
I know I cannot hear His voice
    Upon the shore, nor see Him stand ;
    Yet is it land, ho ! land.

The land ! the land ! the lovely land !
" Far off " dost say ? *Far off*—ah, blessed home !
Farewell ! farewell ! thou salt sea-foam !
    Ah, keel upon the silver sand—
    Land, ho ! land.

You cannot see the land, my land,
You cannot see, and yet the land is there—
My land, my land, through murky air—
    I did not say 'twas close at hand—
    But—land, ho ! land.

Dost hear the bells of my sweet land,
Dost hear the kine, dost hear the merry birds?
No voice, 'tis true, no spoken words,
    No tongue that thou may'st understand—
    Yet is it land, ho ! land.

It's clad in purple mist, my land,
In regal robe it is apparelled,
A crown is set upon its head,
    And on its breast a golden band—
    Land, ho ! land.

Dost wonder that I long for land?
My land is not a land as others are—
Upon its crest there beams a star,
    And lilies grow upon the strand—
    Land, ho ! land.

Give me the helm ! there is the land !
Ha ! lusty mariners, she takes the breeze !
And what my spirit sees it sees
    Leap, bark, as leaps the thunderbrand -
    Land, ho ! land.

PRAESTO

Expecting Him my door was open wide :
   Then I looked round
   If any lack of service might be found,
And saw Him at my side :—
   How entered, by what secret stair,
   I know not, knowing only He was there.

EVENSONG

EASTWARD the valley of my soul was lit
  This morning: now the West hath laid
    Upon its fields the festal robe,
  And East hath shade.
Full soon the night shall fit
  Her star besprinkled serge
    On hill, and rock, and bay;
      But even then behind the mounting globe
  God makes a verge
    Of dawn that shall be day.

POETS AND POETS

HE fishes in the night of deep sea pools
    For him the nets hang long and low,
Cork-buoyed and strong ; the silver-gleaming schools
    Come with the ebb and flow
Of universal tides, and all the channels glow.

Or holding with his hand the weighted line
    He sounds the languor of the neaps,
Or feels what current of the springing brine
    The cord divergent sweeps,
The throb of what great heart bestirs the middle deeps.

Thou also weavest meshes, fine and thin,
    And leaguer'st all the forest ways ;
But of that sea and the great heart therein
    Thou knowest nought : whole days
Thou toil'st, and hast thy end—good store of pies and jays

OPIFEX

As I was carving images from clouds,
    And tinting them with soft ethereal dyes
    Pressed from the pulp of dreams, one comes, and
        cries—
"Forbear!" and all my heaven with gloom enshrouds.

"Forbear! Thou hast no tools wherewith to essay
    The delicate waves of that elusive grain:
    Wouldst have due recompence of vulgar pain?
The potter's wheel for thee, and some coarse clay!

"So work, if work thou must, O humbly skilled!
    Thou hast not known the Master; in thy soul
    His spirit moves not with a sweet control;
Thou art outside, and art not of the guild."

Thereat I rose, and from his presence passed,

    But, going, murmured—"To the God above,

    Who holds my heart, and knows its store of love,

I turn from thee, thou proud iconoclast."

Then on the shore God stooped to me, and said—

    "He spake the truth ; even so the springs are set

    That move thy life, nor will they suffer let,

Nor change their scope, else, living, thou wert dead.

"This is thy life : indulge its natural flow ;

    And carve these forms : they yet may find a place

    On shelves for them reserved : in any case,

I bid thee carve them, knowing what I know."

A MORNING WALK

"Lie there," I said, "my sorrow! lie thou there!
And I will drink the lissome air,
   And see if yet the heavens have gained their blue."
Then rose my Sorrow as an aged man,
And stared, as such a one will stare,
A querulous doubt through tears that freshly ran :
   Wherefore I said—"Content ! thou shalt go too."

So went we through the sunlit crocus-glade,
I and my Sorrow, casting shade
   On all the innocent things that upward pree,
And coax for smiles : but, as I went, I bowed,
And whispered—"Be no whit afraid !
He will pass sad and gentle as a cloud
   It is my Sorrow ; leave him unto me."

And every flowcret in that happy place
Yearned up into the weary face
  With pitying love, and held its golden breath,
Regardless seeming he, as though within
Was nothing apt for their sweet grace,
Nor any sense save such as is akin
  To charnel glooms and emptiness of death.

Then sung a lusty bird, whose throat was clear
And strong with elemental cheer,
  Till very heaven seemed lifted with the joy:
Jet after jet tumultuous music burst
Fount-like, and filled the expanding sphere ;
Whereat my soul was fain to slake its thirst,
  Intent, and ravished with that blest employ.

The songster ceased :—articulate as a bell
The rippling echoes fell and fell
  Upon the shore of silence.   Then I turned
To call upon my Sorrow—he was not ;
But oh what splendour filled the dell !
There ! there ! oh there ! upon the very spot
  Where he had been an awful glory burned.

It was as though the mouth of God had kissed
And purpled into amethyst
    Wan lips, as though red-quickening ichor rills
Had flushed his heart : 'Twas he no more, no more !
'Twas *she*, my soul's evangelist,
My rose, my love, and lovelier than before,
    Dew-nurtured on the far Celestial hills.

"O love," I cried, " I come, I come to thee !
Stay ! stay !"   But softly, silently,
    As pales the moon before the assault of day,
So, spectral-white against the brighter blue,
Faded my darling.   But with me
Walks never more that shadow.   God is true,
    And God was in that bird, believe it as ye may.

IN MEMORIAM J. MACMEIKIN

DIED *April* 1883

EXCELLENT Manxman, Scotia gave you birth,

    But you were ours, being apt to take the print

    Of island forms, the mood, the tone, the tint ;

    Nor missed the ripples of the larger mirth :

A lovely soul has sought the silent firth ;

    Yet haply on our shores you still may hint

    A delicate presence, though no visible dint

    Betrays where you have touched the conscious earth.

You walk with our loved " Chalse " ; you help him speak

    A gracious tongue, to us not wholly clear,

    And sing the " Hymns "—fond dream that wont to dwell

In his confusion.   Friend of all things weak,

    Go down to that sweet soil you held so dear !

Go up to God, and joys unspeakable !

"GOD IS LOVE"

At Derby Haven in the sweet Manx land
A little girl had written on the sand
This legend—"God is love." But, when I said—
"What means this writing?" thus she answered--
"It's father that's at 'say,'
And I come here to pray,
And . . . God is love." My eyes grew dim—
Blest child! in Heaven above
Your angel sees the face of Him
Whose name is love.

THE INTERCEPTED SALUTE

A LITTLE maiden met me in the lane,
And smiled a smile so very fain,
So full of trust and happiness,
I could not choose but bless
The child, that she should have such grace
To laugh into my face.

She never could have known me : but I thought
It was the common joy that wrought
Within the little creature's heart,
As who should say—"Thou art
As I : the heaven is bright above us ;
And there is God to love us.
And I am but a little gleeful maid,
And thou art big, and old, and staid ;

But the blue hills have made thee mild
As is a little child.
Wherefore I laugh that thou may'st see—
Oh laugh! O laugh with me!"

A pretty challenge!   Then I turned me round,
And straight the sober truth I found :
For I was not alone ; behind me stood,
Beneath his load of wood,
He that of right the smile possessed —
Her father manifest.

Oh blest be God! that such an overplus
Of joy is given to us ;
That that sweet innocent
Gave me the gift she never meant,
A gift secure and permanent ;
For, howsoe'er the smile had birth,
It is an added glory on the earth.

ΜΕΤΑΒΟΛΗ

THE fashions change, for change is dear to men ;
    " Πάντων γλυκύτατον μεταβολή,"
Opined the Greek who had the widest ken—
    " Change of all things that be
Is sweetest." Yet since Leda's egg swans strive
    To innovate no curvature on that,
And gannets dive as Noah saw them dive
    O'er sunken Ararat.

CATHERINE KINRADE

["ANOTHER unfortunate creature was soon afterwards subjected to the same treatment, although it was admitted she had 'a degree of unsettledness and defect of understanding,' and, as was certified by the clergy, that she had submitted 'with as much submission and discretion as can be expected of the like of her,' and 'considering the defect of her understanding.' The records state - ' Forasmuch as neither Christian advice nor gentle modes of punishment are found to have any effect on Kath. Kinred of Kirk Christ, a notorious strumpet, who had brought forth three illegitimate children, and still continues to stroll about the country, and lead a most vicious and scandalous life on other _ counts; all which tending to the great dishonour of the Christian name, and to her own utter destruction without a timely and thorough reformation. It is therefore hereby ordered (as well for the further punishment of the said delinquent as for the example of others) that he and Kath. Kinred be dragged after a boat in the sea at Peel, on Wed., the 17th inst. (being the fair of St. Patrick's, at the height of the market. To which end, a boat and boat's crew are to be charged by the general sumner, and the constable and soldiers of the garrison are, by the Governor's order, to be aiding and assisting in seeing this order performed. And in case any owner, master, or crew of any ... are found refractory, by refusing or neglecting to perform this ... for the restraining of vice, their names are to be forthwith given ... the general sumner, to the end they may be severally fined for that contempt, as the Governor's order directs. Dated at Bishop's Court this 15th day of March, 1713.

THOS. SODOR AND MAN.
'WILLIAM WALKER.'

" It was certified by the Sumner General so long after as July 13th ensuing, that ' St. Patrick's day being so stormy and tempestuous that no boat could perform the within censure, upon St. German's day about the height of the market the within Kath. Kinred was dragged after a boat in the sea according to the within order.' However, poor Katherine Kinred is not yet done with, for on the 27th Oct., 1718, having had a fourth bastard child, and 'after imprisonment, penance, dragging in the sea, continuing still remorseless,' and notwithstanding her ' defect of understanding,' she is again ' ordered to be twenty-one days closely imprisoned, and (as soon as the weather will permit) dragged in the sea again after a boat, and also perform public penance in all the churches of this island.' After undergoing all this, she is apparently penitent, 'according to her capacity,' and is ordered by the Bishop 'to be received into the peace of the Church, according to the forms appointed for that purpose.' 'Given under my hand this 13th day of Aug., 1720.' "

See *Manx Society's Publications*, vol. xi. pp. 98, 99.]

NONE spake when Wilson stood before

    The throne—

  And He that sat thereon

Spake not ; and all the presence-floor

Burnt deep with blushes, as the angels cast

Their faces downwards—Then at last,

    Awe-stricken, he was ware

  How on the emerald stair

A woman sat divinely clothed in white,

And at her knees four cherubs bright,

    That laid

Their heads within her lap.   Then, trembling, he essayed
    To speak   "Christ's mother, pity me!"
    Then answered she—
"Sir, I am Catherine Kinrade."

Even so--the poor dull brain,
    Drenched in unhallowed fire,
It had no vigour to restrain
    God's image trodden in the mire
Of impious wrongs   whom last he saw
Gazing with animal awe
Before his harsh tribunal, proved unchaste,
Incorrigible, woman's form defaced
To uttermost ruin by no fault of hers
So gave her to the torturers.
And now   some vital spring adjusted,
Some faculty that rusted
Cleansed to legitimate use
Some undeveloped action stirred, some juice
Of God's distilling dropt into the core
Of all her life   no more
In that dark grave entombed,

Her soul had bloomed

To perfect woman—woman made to honour,

With all the glory of her youth upon her.

And from her lips and from her eyes there flowed

    A smile that lit all Heaven—the angels smiled ;

God smiled, if that were smile beneath the state that glowed

    Soft purple—and a voice—" Be reconciled ! "

So to his side the children crept,

And Catherine kissed him, and he wept.

Then said a seraph—" Lo ! he is forgiven."

And for a space again there was no voice in Heaven.

NATURE AND ART

1

I once loved Nature so that man was nought
    And nought the works of man,
Whether the human force that inward wrought
    My vital needs outran,
    And, bidden by great Pan,
In its all-quickening arms the visible deadness caught

Or was it accident of time and place?
    For men were few to see
Where I was reared, and Nature's copious grace
    Of form and colour free
    Eclipsed the piety
Of childish social loves, and motions of the race—

I know not quite : but this to me is known,

    That, with a soft unrest,

Soul unto soul in perfect aptness grown,

    I drew her to my breast,

    A personal creature pressed,

Full of a passionate will, and moods that were her own.

Her own, yet, modulate and tuned to mine,

    She shaped her meek replies

So that I ne'er bethought me to divine

    If in her wondrous eyes

    A light congenial lies,

Or, sprung from alien blood, insensate glories shine.

If homogeneous with me or not

    The question never tried me,

Or when, or wherefore, or of whom begot,

    She seemed to stand outside me,

    To soothe me and to guide me,

Another, or myself reflex, who cared one jot ?

Thrice blest if I might roam on fell or shore
    In exquisite solitude,
And uncontrolled the ὀαριστύς pour
    That with its interlude,
    Far from all discord rude,
Comes once to fresh young hearts, and comes not evermore.

Oh poet flush of all-compelling youth !
    Oh great interpreter !
Oh artist prescient of the higher truth !
    Oh confident Lucifer !
    Oh nobly prone to err !
Oh shadowless of doubt, oh innocent of ruth !

Oh instinct vast ! oh indiscriminate mind !
    Not thus, but hesitant long,
That sculptor won the marble to be kind ;
    Thus rather, right or wrong
    Untaught, Ixion strong
Held Nephele in arms a god might not unbind.

Then came the interact of will on will
  The monad soul to frame ;
And I was one of many, passion still,
  And use, and praise, and blame,
  The different, the same,
Shaping the definite self with change of good and ill.

A man with other men I had to dwell ;
  I had to love and hate,
To traffic with my heart, to buy and sell
  Love's wares at current rate,
  Mine enemies in the gate
With keen-edged sword of speech to harass and to quell.

Wherefore I come a being manifold,
  Nature, to sue thy grace ;
It is not that my heart is growing cold,
  If, conscious of my race,
  I look into thy face
With a less simple trust than that I felt of old.

It is because thou seem'st at our alarms
    Unmoved : the ages fall
Helpless from out the rigour of thine arms,
    Thou heeding not at all
    If bridal veil or pall
Illustrate or obscure the glory of thy charms.

It is because, with all thy loveliness,
    Thou hast no delicate flush
Of feeling instant in its brimmed excess,
    And rippled at the brush
    Of lightest thought : the hush
Is thine of ordered change, fixed and emotionless.

It is because thou canst not apprehend
    Beyond our simplest needs,
Because, obedient to thy native end,
    Thou knowest only deeds
    Where link to link succeeds,
And no irrational gaps the golden sequence rend.

It is because the tracks of errant souls
  Appear to thee so straight,
Unskilled to mark how latent force controls
  The bias and the rate,
  How inward grasping fate
Collects the various lines, and diverse sends the bowls.

Moreover, all the things that men have done
  The things that men have said,
Have made another light beneath the sun,
  Another darkness shed,
  Another soul-stream fed,
To cool in other wells, o'er other weirs to run.

I grant thou hast the very notes of prime,
  But of the thousand tunes
Wherewith our summer loads the growing time,
  The joyaunce of our Junes,
  The full chromatic noons,
There is no scale to fit thy diapason chime.

Nor wilt thou, kindly monished, recognise
      Of life the complex game :
We are not now as when, 'neath kindlier skies
        Begot, to that great dame
        Th' auroral offspring came :
We are no babes astride upon Eve's awful thighs.

So, haply, one has known a foster-sister,
        And, when the years have gone,
Has felt, with all his hopes, as if he missed her,
        And come, and looked upon
        Her face, and proved anon
Her eyes were meaningless, and, sadly silent, kissed her.

II

Oh Heaven ! the mannikin ! Is this gratitude ?
      "A foster sister," saidst thou ?
"A complex game ? " What fell Locusta stewed
        That damned fucus ? Spread'st thou
        The stuff upon thee ? wed'st thou
That specious harlotry from Hell's black bosom spewed ?

Up, up! for shame! She is thy sister : love her,

    Come to her yet again :

Think not thine own quintessenced self above her !

    Oh see how she is fain

    Her shyness to explain !

Oh ! understand the blush her virgin cheek doth cover !

Eve, Adam ! Yes, and all that Eden sap—

    Is it impossible ?

'Twould do thee good to lie in her great lap,

    To have thy utmost will,

    To fill thy utmost fill,

Creamed from the copious duct of that primeval pap.

Thou talk'st of music, and of tunes accord

    With specialties to flirt—

What wouldst thou have? a homily—good lord !

    A logic malapert,

    With pretty fence expert,

The play of thy caprice infallible to ward ?

O fool! O fool!   This is the very acme;

  Far far within the cells

Of winding thought where man may never track me

  She takes me, and she tells

  The quaintest things, and spells

Ineffable spirit-tunes, and lulls the cares that rack me.

O twilight bliss!   O happy even-song!

  How well I know thy power!

O heather bells, that peal your faint ding-dong!

  O bee in sunny hour

  Urging from flower to flower

The shrill-resounding brass of thy most patient gong!

O prelude of the windy-wailing morn!

  O long drawn moorland whistle!

O rustling of the multitudinous corn!

  O sough of reed or thistle!

  O holy, holy missal

Intoned by hooded clouds! oh joy that I was born!

But thou'rt a being manifold—alack !

    And tak'st the simple sense

Into thy crucible, and giv'st it back

    Brain-filtered and intense,

    And Nature is too dense

Forsooth ! to hit thy scope, and imitate the knack !

Nay, what is this thou of thyself hast made ?

    Is this *development* ?

O Lord of all the souls ! is this the trade

    For which we here were sent ?

    Is't not an accident,

By-play of function-work, by casual contact swayed ?

'Tis not essential, though the world is roomy,

    That I should coexist

With any animal *bipes implume*,

    It is the core and gist

    Of life that I should list

To Nature's voice alone, and hearken if she woo me.

But, as it is, innumerous bipeds press
    And crowd on one another,
Nor would I have one animal the less,
    And I must know my brother,
    Some odd misgivings smother,
And smile, and chat, and take my commons with the mess.

Of course, the absolutest slave that crawls
    Is social: so am I:
I have a place, I live within four walls
    Even horse to horse will try
    Some matter of reply,
And hear his neighbour munch, and whinny o'er the stalls.

But this is accident, casual relation,
    Wholly subordinate
To the main purport of our earthly station,
    Which is to permeate
    One soul with fullest freight
Of constant natural forms, not factual complication.

Else were our life both frivolous and final,

  A mere skiomachy,

Not succulent of growth, not officinal

  To what shall after be,

  But Fortune's devilry

Of Harlequin with smirk theatro-columbinal—

A changeling life, that to the world's great heart

  Just leans its elfish lips,

And soon falls off, and dies an imp confest,

  And seeks the void, and skips,

  As the dull Fury whips

The ineffectual ghosts, and drives it with the rest.

And, if the man has 'scaped such inanition,

  Then why, returning here,

Does he not speak the language of contrition,

  And strip the base veneer

  From his poor soul, and fear,

And seek the long-lost love that saved him from perdition?

What means this talk of "complex game," and matters

    That she "cannot divine"?

I tear this wretched sham of his to tatters:

    O blessed nature-wine!

    O sacred anodyne!

He is fact-poisoned, he! and knows not what he chatters.

Let him come humbly, let him make confession

    It is no fault of hers

If he is all too dull to catch th' expression

    Of her great thought, or blurs

    Its mobile signatures

With mediate glare of self, and balks the true possession.

O sweet Titania, bedded in the cities!

    I hate to think of it

Pranking that ass's head with daffodillies,

    That in his puzzled wit

    Knows not thou art more fit

To hold in odorous arms the Peleid Achilles!

And yet he says, his lip fastidious-curled,

     "She's unappreciative."

Take him, good Puck, I prythee have him hurled

     To where he is more native,

     To chums communicative—

Snout, Snug, the parish club he fondly calls the world.

For me the happiness—my good I find

     In Nature's energies,

And am not frustrate.   Nature is not blind

     In promptings such as these,

     But holds the secret keys

Wherewith the wards that fence our hope she can unwind.

Both wrong, both right.   'Tis God appoints our state—

     Nature and art are one—

True art, true nature, never separate

     In things beneath the sun.

     So is His pleasure done

Who moulds the wills of men, and grasps the bars of fate.

LIFE

O LIFE of man, if life 'tis meet to call
This rolling with a rolling ball
Some seventy periods round the sun,
O life that only art to have begun
A life, then straight art not a life at all.

O rigid curve mechanical,
If thou wert only absolute,
If all our energies were summed in thee,
If one great pathos thrilled the iron ring,
If, points upon the circle, fixed and mute,
We felt the dominant spring
And strain of power, then were it blest to be—

Not death would all be death, if, truly free,

We had the motion of the sphere,

If no quick atom jarred

Oblique, and crossed the act divine,

And vexed the loyal round with idiot cheer

Of self, and scrabbled all the line

With zigzags of the will, and kindly oneness marred.

JESSIE

WHEN Jessie comes with her soft breast,

 And yields the golden keys,

Then is it as if God caressed

 Twin babes upon His knees

Twin babes that, each to other pressed,

Just feel the Father's arms, wherewith they both are blessed.

But when I think if we must part,

 And all this personal dream be fled

Oh then my heart ! oh then my useless heart !

 Would God that thou wert dead

A clod insensible to joys or ills

A stone remote in some bleak gully of the hills !

ALMA MATER

O MOTHER Earth, by the bright sky above thee,
I love thee, oh I love thee !
And yet they say that I must leave thee soon ;
    And if it must be so,
Then to what sun or moon
    Or star I am to go,
    Or planet, matters not for me to know.
O mother Earth, by the bright sky above thee,
I love thee, oh I love thee !

Oh whither will you send me,
Oh wherefore will you rend me
    From your warm bosom, mother mine—
I can't fix my affections
On a state of conic sections,

And I don't care how old Daedalus
May try to coax and wheedle us
With wings he manufactures,
Sure to end in compound fractures,
    Or in headers at right-angles to the brine
O mother Earth, by the bright sky above thee,
I love thee, oh I love thee!

    I cannot leave thee, mother;
    I love thee, and not another;
    And I can't say "man and brother"
    To a shadowy abstraction,
    To an uncomfortable fraction,
    To the skeletons of quiddities,
    And similar stupidities.
    Have mercy, mother, mercy!
    The unjustest of *novercæ*
    Sometimes leaves off her snarlings
    At her predecessor's darlings;
    And thou art *all* my mother,
    I know not any other.
O mother Earth, by the bright sky above thee,
I love thee, oh I love thee!

So let me leave thee never,

But cling to thee for ever,

And hover round thy mountains,

And flutter round thy fountains

    And pry into thy roses fresh and red ;

And blush in all thy blushes,

And flush in all thy flushes,

And watch when thou art sleeping,

And weep when thou art weeping,

And be carried with thy motion,

As the rivers and the ocean,

As the great rocks and the trees are

And all the things one sees are—

O mother, this were glorious life,

    This were not to be dead.

O mother Earth, by the bright sky above thee,

I love thee, oh I love thee !

TRITON ESURIENS

How cold and hungry is the sea to-day,
    How clamorous against the thrifty shore,
    That yields not of her store
Save sands, and weeds, and pebbles of the bay!
    "Give more! give more!"
Methinks I hear him say;
"And drive the hunger of my heart away!

"Give me of sunny flowers, of golden grain,
    Of meadows sopped with sippings of the dew;
    Small loss it were to you,
To me great solace of my endless pain;
    For few! ah few!
And shadowy and vain
The joys that haunt my solitary reign!

"'Take me for ever to your constant breast,

 O land, O lovely, most unchanging land !

 Can you not understand

How all my restlessness desires your rest ?

 What murderer's brand

Is stamped by God's behest

Upon this brow, that you should loathe my quest ?

"O mute, insensate land ! nor voiceless she,

 For she can speak, and I have heard her speak,

 When zephyrs kissed her cheek,

Love-whispering in the twilight on the lea ;

 Then, hushed, and meek,

I've heard her gentle glee,

And schooled my heart to think 'twas not for me.

"Sometimes at evening I have heard you pray,

 And listened, looking up the misty glen,

 And only said *Amen*,

Else silent, lest one sound uncaught should stray ;

 And then, oh then !

' Our Father,' you did say;

But I have been a wanderer wild alway.

"Oh I am hungry, hungry at my heart !

    Give me, oh give me, even of thy worst !

    Give, as to one accurst,

Drear moorlands, and all rushy fens, where start

    Black streams, that, nurst

In barrenness, must part !

Give me but wastes and snippets of the chart ! "

Thus speaks the sea, his hue all ashen gray

    With paleness of inveterate desires ;

    Then on the ebb retires—

Full strange it seems that that cold heart should sway

    With passionate fires !

But ah ! my soul can say

How vain it is when she requires

The coast, so near, yet on whose absolute spires

Looms the sad frown of an eternal " Nay."

THE PEEL LIFE-BOAT

Of Charley Cain, the cox,
And the thunder of the rocks,
And the ship St. George,
How he balked the sea-wolf's gorge
Of its prey—
Southward bound from Norraway ;
And the fury and the din,
And the horror and the roar,
Rolling in, rolling in,
Rolling in upon the dead lee-shore.

See the Harbour-master stands,
Cries—-" Have you all your hands ? "
Then, as an angel springs
With God's breath upon his wings,

She went :
And the black storm robe was rent
With the shout and with the din
And the horror and the roar
Rolling in, rolling in,
Rolling in upon the dead lee-shore.

And the castle walls were crowned,
And no woman lay in swound,
But they stood upon the height
Straight and stiff to see the fight,
For they knew
What the pluck of men can do
With the fury and the din
And the horror and the roar, etc.

" Lay aboard her, Charley lad ! "
" Lay aboard her ! Are you mad ?
With the bumping and the scamper
Of all this loose deck hamper,
And the yards
Dancing round us here like cards,
With the fury and the din, etc.

So Charley scans the rout,

Charley knows what he's about,

Keeps his distance, heaves the line—

" Pay it out there true and fine !

Not too much, men !

Take in the slack, you Dutchmen !"

With the fury, etc.

Now the hauser's fast and steady,

And the traveller rigged and ready.

Says Charley—" What's the lot ? "

" Twenty-four."   Then like a shot—

" Twenty-three,"

Says Charley, " 's all I see "—

With the fury, etc.

" Not a soul shall leave the wreck,"

Says Charley, " till on deck

You bring the man that's hurt."

So they brought him in his shirt- -

Oh it's fain

I am for you, Charles Cain—

With the fury, etc.

And the Captain and his wife,
And a baby! odds my life!
Such a beauty! such a prize!
And the tears in Charley's eyes.
Arms of steel,
For the honour of old Peel
Haul away amid the din, etc.

Sing ho! the seething foam!
Sing ho! the road for home!
And the hulk they've left behind,
Like a giant stunned and blind
With the loom
And the boding of his doom
With the fury, etc.

" Here's a child! don't let it fall!"
Says Charley, " Nurse it, all!"
Oh the tossing of the breasts!
Oh the brooding of soft nests,

Taking turns,

As each maid and mother yearns

For the babe that scaped the din

And the fury and the roar, etc.

See the rainbow bright and broad !

Now, all men, thank ye God,

For the marvel and the token,

And the word that He hath spoken.

With Thee,

O Lord of all that be,

We have peace amid the din,

And the horror and the roar,

Rolling in, rolling in,

Rolling in upon the dead lee-shore.

Q

A WISH

Of two things one—with Chaucer let me ride,
And hear the Pilgrims' tales : or, that denied,
Let me with Petrarch in a dew-sprent grove
Ring endless changes on the bells of love.

DANTE AND ARIOSTO

If Dante breathes on me his awful breath,
I rise and go ; but I am sad as death —
I go ; but, turning, who is that I see ?
I whisper " Ariosto, wait for me ' "

BOCCACCIO

Boccaccio, for you laughed all laughs that are—
   The Cynic scoff, the chuckle of the churl,
   The laugh that ripples over reefs of pearl,
   The broad, the sly, the hugely jocular,
Men call you lewd, and coarse, allege you mar
   The music that, withdrawn your ribald skirl,
   Were sweet as note of mavis or of merle—
   Wherefore they frown, and rate you at the bar.

One thing is proved—To count the sad degrees
   Upon the Plague's dim dial, catch the tone
   Of a great death that lies upon a land,
Feel nature's ties, yet hold with steadfast hand
   The diamond, you are three that stand alone—
   You, and Lucretius, and Thucydides.

TO E. M. O.

CHANCE-CHILD of some lone sorrow on the hills
Bach finds a babe: instant the great heart fills
With love of that fair innocence,
Conveys it thence,
Clothes it with all divinest harmonies,
Gives it sure foot to tread the dim degrees
Of Pilate's stair— Hush! hush! its last sweet breath
Wails far along the passages of death.

Time   Eternity

CAROL

THREE kings from out the Orient
For Judah's land were fairly bent,
      To find the Lord of grace ;
And as they journeyed pleasantlie,
A star kept shining in the sky,
      To guide them to the place.
" O Star," they cried, " by all confest,
Withouten dreed the loveliest ! "

The first was Melchior to see,
The emperour hight of Arabye,
      An aged man, I trow :
He sat upon a rouncy bold,
Had taken of the red red gold,
      The babe for to endow.
" O Star," he cried, etc.

The next was Gaspar, young and gay,
That held the realm of far Cathay –
    Our Jesus drew him thence
Yclad in silk from head to heel.
He rode upon a high cameel,
    And bar the frankincense.
"O Star," he cried, etc.

The last was dusky Balthasar,
That rode upon a dromedar
    His coat was of the fur :
Dark-browed he came from Samarkand,
The Christ to seek, and in his hand
    Upheld the bleeding myrrh.
"O Star," he cried, etc.

ISRAEL AND HELLAS

I SOMETIMES wonder of the Grecian men
    If all that was to them for life appears—
Simple, full-orbed, they float across our ken,
    And to their modern feres
Present the gathered light of all their years.

But was it all—the utmost of their reach—
    That unto us the sedulous scribe has passed—
To carve on marble-slabs of that great speech
    Great thoughts, that so might last—
Was that the single aim their copious souls forecast?

On them, high-strung (for so it seems to us),
    Did no kind god distil a wholesome ease?
Laughed no fair child for good Herodotus?
    Looked there no maiden of the midland seas
Into thy clear gray eyes, Thucydides?

One life, one work—was this to them the all—
    God's purpose marked, and followed fair and true?
Or were they slaves like us, whom doubts enthrall—
    A hesitant, futile crew,
Who know not what our Lord would have us do?

Was mind supreme?   Was animal craving nought?
    Or that the essence? this the accident?
Did it suffice them to have nobly thought?
    And, the whole impulse spent,
Did the vexed waters meet in smoothness of content?

They ate, they drank, they married in the prime,
    And tied their souls with natural, homely needs,
They bowed before the beadles of the time,
    And wore the common weeds,
And fed the priests, and ménaged the creeds.

Or were they happier, breathing social free,
    No smug respectability to pat
And soothe with pledges of equality,
    Ironical, whereat
The goodman glows through all his realms of fat?

And was it possible for them to hold
    A creed elastic in that lightsome air,
And let sweet fables droop in flexile fold
    From off their shoulders bare,
Loose-fitting, jewel-clasped with fancies rare?

For not as yet intense across the sea
    Came the swart Hebrew with a fiery haste;
In long brown arms entwined Euphrosyne,
    And round her snowy waist
Fast bound the Nessus-robe, that may not be displaced.

Yes, this is true; but the whole truth is more;
    This was not all the burning Orient gave;
Through purple partings of her golden door
    Came gleams upon the wave,
Long shafts that search the souls of men who crave;

And probings of the heart, and spirit-balm,
    And to deep questionings the deep replies
That echo in the everlasting calm—
    All this from forth those skies,
Beside Gehenna fire and worm that never dies.

Yet, if the Greek went straighter to his aim,

    If, knowing wholly what he meant to do,

He did it, given circumstance the same,

    Or near the same, then must I hold it true

That from his different creed the vantage came.

    Who, seizing one world where we balance two,

From its great secular heart the readier current drew.

M. T. W.

FAR swept from Lundy, spanned from side to side
  With heaven's blue arch, the ocean waters flow ;
  Sweet May has piled her pyramids of snow,
And the fair land is glorious as a bride
That chooses summer for her hour of pride :
  The lordly sun, with his great heart a-glow,
  Is fain to kiss all things that bud and blow,
And Maurice sleeps, nor hears the murmuring tide.

  Fine spirit, wheresoe'er, a quester keen,
You mark the asphodel with prints of pearl,
  Breathing the freshness of the early lawns,
  O darling, clad in light of tend'rest sheen,
Hard by the nest of some celestial merle
  We yet shall see you when the morning dawns.

DREAMS

It looks as if in dreams the soul was free,
       No bodily limit checks its absolute play ;
Then why doth it not use its liberty,
       And clear a certain way
To further truth beyond the actual sea ?

It is not so ; for when, with loosened grip,
       The warder sense unlocks the visible hold,
Then will my soul from forth its chamber slip,
       An idiot blithe and bold,
And into vacancy of folly skip ;

Or aimless wander on the poppied floor
       Of gaudy fields, or, scared upon the street,
Return unto the grim, familiar door,
       And coward crave retreat,
As who had never been outside before.

What boots it that I hold the chartered space,

    If I but fill it with th' accustomed forms,

And load its breathless essence with the trace

    Of casual-risen storms,

And drag my chain along the lovely place?

Oh but if God would make a deep suspense,

    And draw me perfect from th' adhesive sheath ;

If all the veils and swathings of pretence,

    Dropt from me, sunk beneath,

Then would I get me very far from hence.

I'd come to Him with one swift arrow-dart,

    Aimed at the zenith of th' o'erbrooding blue ;

Straight to the centre of His awful heart

    The flight long-winged and true

Should bear me rapt through all the spheres that part.

But as it is, it is a waste of rest,

    God uses not the occasion : on the rock

Stands prone my soul, a diver lean undrest,

    And looks, and fears the shock,

And turns and hides its shame with some poor sorry jest.

WESLEY IN HEAVEN

When Wesley died, the Angelic orders
    To see him at the state
Pressed so incontinent that the warders
    Forgot to shut the gate.
So I, that hitherto had followed
    As one with grief o'ercast,
Where for the doors a space was hollowed,
    Crept in, and heard what passed.
And God said "Seeing thou hast given
    Thy life to my great sounds,
Choose thou through all the cirque of Heaven
    What most of bliss redounds."
Then Wesley said "I hear the thunder
    Low growling from Thy seat—
Grant me that I may bind it under
    The trampling of my feet."

And Wesley said—"See, lightning quivers
    Upon the presence walls—
Lord, give me of it four great rivers,
    To be my manuals."

And then I saw the thunder chidden
    As slave to his desire,
And then I saw the space bestridden
    With four great bands of fire.

And stage by stage, stop stop subtending,
    Each lever strong and true,
One shape inextricable blending,
    The awful organ grew.

Then certain angels clad the Master
    In very marvellous wise,
Till clouds of rose and alabaster
    Concealed him from mine eyes.

And likest o a dove soft brooding,
    The innocent figure ran ;
So breathed the breath of his preluding,
    And then the fugue began —

Began ; but, to his office turning,
    The porter swung his key ;
Wherefore, although my heart was yearning,

I had to go ; but he
Played on ; and, as I downward clomb,
I heard the mighty bars
Of thunder-gusts that shook heaven's dome,
And moved the balanced stars.

TO E. M. O.

Oakeley, whenas the bass you beat
In that tremendous way,
I still could fancy at your feet
A dreadful lion lay.
Askance he views the petulant scores,
But, when you touch a rib, he roars.

PREPARATION

Hast thou a cunning instrument of play,
    'Tis well; but see thou keep it bright,
And tuned to primal chords, so that it may
    Be ready day and night.
For when He comes thou know'st not, who shall say—
"These virginals are apt"; and try a note,
    And sit, and make sweet solace of delight,
That men shall stand to listen on the way,
    And all the room with heavenly music float.

R

PLANTING

Who would be planted chooseth not the soil
        Or here or there,
            Or loam or peat,
        Wherein he best may grow,
And bring forth guerdon of the planter's toil—
        The lily is most fair,
                But says not " I will only blow
Upon a southern land "; the cedar makes no coil
                What rock shall owe
        The springs that wash his feet :
The crocus cannot arbitrate the foil
        That for its purple radiance is most meet
            Lord, even so
        I ask one prayer,
            The which if it be granted,
        It skills not where
                Thou plantest me, only I would be planted

OBVIAM

I NEEDS must meet him, for he hath beset
    All roads that man do travel, hill and plain ;
        Nor aught that breathes shall pass
Unchallenged of his debt.
But what and if, when I shall whet
    My front to meet him, then, as in a glass,
Darkly, I shall behold that he is twain—
Earthward a mask of jet,
Heavenward a coronet
Sun-flushed with roseate gleams—In any case
    It hardly can be called a mortal pain
    To meet whom met I ne'er shall meet again.

SPECULA

WHEN He appoints to meet thee, go thou forth
    It matters not
If south or north,
    Bleak waste or sunny plot.
Nor think, if haply He thou seek'st be late,
    He does thee wrong :
To stile or gate
    Lean thou thy head, and long !
It may be that to spy thee He is mounting
    Upon a tower,
Or in thy counting
    Thou hast mista'en the hour.
But, if He come not, neither do thou go
    Till Vesper chime :
Belike thou then shalt know
    He hath been with thee all the time.

"SOCIAL SCIENCE"

O HAPPY souls, that mingle with your kind,
    That laugh with laughers, weep with weepers,
Whom use gregarious to your like can bind,
    Who sow with sowers, reap with reapers—
  To me it is not known—
  The gentle art to moan
With moaners, wake with wakers, sleep with sleepers.

It must be good to think the common thought,
    To learn with learners, teach with teachers ;
To hold the adjusted soul till it is brought
    To pray with prayers, preach with preachers.
  But I can never catch
  The dominant mode, nor match
The tone, and whine with whiners, screech with screechers.

R*

Yet surely there is warmth, if we combine
    And loaf with loafers, hunt with hunters :
It is a comfort as of nozzling swine
    To row with rowers, punt with punters—
    How is it then that I
    Am alien to the stye,
Nor ever swill with swillers, grunt with grunters ?

I cannot choose but think it is a blessing
    To fool with fools, to scheme with schemers ;
To feel another's arms your soul caressing,
    To sigh with sighers, dream with dreamers—
    But I can't hit the span,
    The regulation man,
Ephemer decent with his coephemers.

Yet, after all, if frustrate of this pleasure,
    To eat with eaters, drink with drinkers,
If I can't find the Greatest Common Measure,
    And cheat with cheaters, wink with winkers,
    At any rate the struggle
    My truer self to juggle,

And force my mind to fit

The standard ell of wit,

Shall never dwarf nor cramp me,

Shall never stint nor scamp me

So that I bleat with bleaters, slink with slinkers.

Thus spake I once, with fierce self-gratulation,

 Nor hoped with hopers, feared with fearers ;

Yet, discontent, it seemed a mere privation

 To doubt with doubters, sneer with sneerers :

 It seemed more happiness

 A brother's hand to press,

To talk with talkers, hear with hearers.

Wherefore, albeit I know it is not great

 Mobbing with mobs, believing with believers,

Yet for the most it is a snugger state

 To gain with gainers, grieve with grievers,

 Than, desolate on a peak,

 To whet one's lonely beak,

And watch the beaver huddling with the beavers.

But though this boon denied, my soul, love thou
    The lover, gibe not with the giber!
O ragged soul! I cannot piece thee now
    That, thread to thread, and fibre unto fibre,
Thou with another soul
Shouldst make a sentient whole :
    But I am proud thou dost retain
    Some tinct of that imperial *murex* grain
No carrack ever bore to Thames or Tiber.

AT THE PLAY

As in a theatre the amusëd sense

    Beholds the strange vicissitudes of things,

    Young Damon's loves, the fates of clowns and kings,

    And all the motley of the gay pretence—

Beholds, and on an acme of suspense

    Stands vibrant till the curtain falls, door swings,

    Lights gutter, and the weary murmurings

    Of o'er-watched varlets intimate us thence—

Even so we gaze not on the things that are,

    Nor aught behold but what is adumbrate :

    The show is specious, and we laugh and weep

At what is only meant spectacular :

    And when the curtain falls, we may not wait :

    Death takes the lights, and we go home to sleep.

Printed by R. & R. CLARK, *Edinburgh.*

www.ingramcontent.com/pod-product-compliance
Lightning Source LLC
Chambersburg PA
CBHW030642030726
47497CB00006B/1919